Tom went over to him. It was an easy choice. Dropping to his knees in front of the Latino's chair, he reached for the buttons of his fly and carefully opened them, while Will opened the last bottle of beer. "Yeah, that's it, Blondie. Nice and gentle, nice and polite. Get it out, man, and get it in."

He took a long drink as Tom breathed in the heady scent of a hot man and reached into the folds of the jeans....

MUSCLE BOUND

CHRISTOPHER MORGAN

A BADBOY BOOK

First BADBOY Edition 1992

First printing May 1992

ISBN 1-56333-028-8

Cover Photograph © 1992 Daniel Perry
Cover Design by Eduardo Andino

Manufactured in the United States of America
Published by Masquerade Books, Inc.
801 Second Avenue
New York, N.Y. 10017

INTRODUCTION

Early Autumn.

The man on the weight machine could only be described as darkly beautiful. Many men (and more then a few women) had told Will Rodriguez that he was handsome, masculine and almost feral in his attractiveness, but it went deeper than that. His sculpted, deeply tanned body was truly a work of art, a type of classic Latin beauty that attracted attention and sexual hunger.

It was no accident that he was like this. As he went into his last series of reps, sweat trickled down his body in rivulets that spilled into the towel he had laid down to catch them, a towel already nearly soaked. His curly black hair was plastered around his head and face, and his muscles strained with the effort he was putting forth. He was clad only in his workout boots, the weight gloves, and a pair of hip-hugging shorts. The tank top was crumpled under his neck to catch the sweat there.

Each time he pressed the bar and raised it, his stomach muscles contracted and rippled, and his chest rose and fell with the rhythm. He was so engrossed in his workout that he didn't notice the door to the private room opening and shutting, admitting a spectator. All of his concentration was on finishing this set, putting the finishing touches on this workout, getting really pumped up.

Some called it obsession, the behavior of those men who sought perfection in their bodies. But it was far more than that. For an obsession is a useless thing, a compulsion to do something because it fills some emotional void. The sculpting of one's body, however, fills many purposes. It keeps you healthy and strong. It makes you attractive and desirable. And in Will's case, it made his prices much, much higher. For services that were very much in demand.

The bar rose and fell. His breath came in harsh whistles between clenched teeth. A lesser man would have given up before the series was finished, but Will stuck to his regimen, and got in his last dozen with a passion that was almost furious. He cried out at the last one, a sound of angry triumph, and relaxed back against the bench, allowing his arms to come to rest at last. A tremble ran through his shoulders and upper arms, and he forced himself to lie still until it washed through him.

The sound of his spectator's voice was not as surprising as it might have been. "Good workout, Willie."

Will cringed at the diminutive and grunted a response. With his right hand, he reached for the squeeze bottle next to the machine and brought it up, just holding it. He took several deep breaths, not responding to the voice.

"I'm glad to see you're sticking to the plan I outlined. I promised you results if you did everything I said, didn't I?" The voice was insistent and thick with sarcasm. Something in it demanded a response, and tension began to curl in the space between the two men, one lying back, the other standing.

The beautiful young man drew himself up to a sitting position and nodded, bringing the straw from the squeeze bottle to his lips. He avoided looking at his visitor in a way that suggested that the squeeze bottle held his attention as much as the workout had.

"Stand up, Willie. Let's see that new body." The attitude was pure authority, no cajoling, no joking. Will put the bottle down and stood up, drops of sweat falling off his arms and trickling down his face. He wiped some of it away with his crumpled tank top, and then stood free of the weight machine.

Will stood 5'8" in his workout boots, but his compact muscular frame compensated for the two additional inches he would have preferred. He finally had the washboard stomach so admired by other men, and there was a fluid grace in the way he moved his body. He knew he was hot. But his posture before the spectator was almost designed to minimize his attractiveness. He stood with his head hung, his arms limp at his sides.

The other man laughed out loud and allowed

that laugh to drain into a sneer. "Don't give me this shit, Willie boy. When I want to see your body, I want to *see* it, sweetie. Get those arms up! Show me some hip! Flex! Now!" He snapped his fingers and moved closer. "Show me what kind of a man I made out of you, you cheap greaser punk!"

"Mr. Marcus, I'm not really in the mood.... I had a real tough workout today, and I gotta get home." Will said this in a dispassionate voice, continuing to avoid the eyes of the spectator. His teeth were clenched as he said it, his shoulders slightly tensed, but he made no move in response to the demands or the insults.

"I don't give a rat's ass what mood you're in, Willie boy. Moods are for girls, aren't they? Now, are you going to do what I said, or am I going to have to teach you a lesson?"

There was a long moment as the two men stood in silence. The room was thick with the smells of masculine labor, old and new sweat and the musky odor of sexual release. Will imagined that he could see the smells, mingling with the bleach and disinfectants. He stood until the silence grew to be oppressive, and just as Mr. Marcus was about to walk toward him again, he lifted his arms and struck a pose.

If his body was a classic, so was his training. He mutely went through a series of bodybuilder poses that showed him off to his best advantage, holding each pose for about ten seconds before curling into another one.

"Good boy," Mr. Marcus said, coming even closer. "That's it, keep your head up. Round those shoulders a little more, show off those nice tits. They look better now we've got that dipshit hair off, don't they?" And when Will refused to respond, Marcus lifted one hand warningly. "Answer me, you scumbag!"

"Yeah!" Will spat, coming out of his pose. "Yeah, they look better."

Marcus laughed. "Get those fucking shorts off."

Will released the cord in the waistband and dropped the soft, damp garment to the floor, where he stepped out of them. He had no tan line. The same caramel color that covered his chest extended down around his cock. Even his dick was a creamy brown, uncut and curved down over his balls, cradled in a wiry nest of damp black pubic hair.

"Good." Marcus snapped his fingers again. "Do it again. This time, make me hard." He cupped one massive hand over his crotch and nodded for Will to start posing.

This time, Will's efforts were more concentrated. It was a different set of poses too, more sexually charged, slower. His tan skin barely hid the flushes of embarrassment he felt as he turned and bent over, sliding his hands down one muscular leg, and then the other, exposing his rounded cheeks to the man who had compelled his obedience. Finally, as he reached for his cock and balls, to hold them and display them as though they too were part of his bodybuilding development, Marcus opened the fly of his jeans and brought his machine out.

Because that was how Will saw it and thought of it. It wasn't a dick, or a prick, or a cock. It was no dong, no tool. It was a *machine*, capable of doing things no other man's meat could match, and even as he gripped his own manhood in his hands, he was stunningly aware of how inadequate it was compared to the thing that Marcus was displaying.

"Get over here and do what you were born to, punk. Get your mouth on some real meat and take it down."

Will dropped to his knees and let his cock and balls go free. Slowly, he took hold of the cock before him and licked his lips, and then lowered his face over the tip. The head fit into his mouth, a fat, silken ball, and Marcus pressed into him relentlessly. Will closed his eyes.

"That's my boy, take it down. You know you want it, don't you, you fucking little spic … just like you did the first night, huh? Come on, let me feel your tongue, that's it, suck on it. Think now that you've got a real body you're some kind of man, huh? Not with me, you fairy punk, you're still my fuckhole, aren't you?"

Marcus began to rock his hips back and forth, and when Will tried to pull away, he grabbed a handful of curly black hair and ground his crotch into Will's face ruthlessly, not pulling back until Will's body began to fight the lack of air. Then, Marcus pulled way back and slammed forcefully into Will's throat.

"Don't even *think* of trying to get away from me, Willie baby. You remember that you agreed to this? You're gonna be my good fuckhole, and I'm gonna make a man out of you, right? You remember that, don't you? Cheap ten dollar blowjob trick, you never even saw a real man until you met me. And you'll never be man enough to take me on, fucker. Got that? Never!"

Will struggled, but not to get away. He struggled to get in a deep breath in between Marcus' deep thrusts. He made no more attempts to please the man, just to keep his mouth and throat open, and to keep his lips closed around the massive shaft.

Finally, Marcus pulled his machine out of Will's mouth. Using one hand, he milked the shaft, and growled instructions. "Arch your back! Spread those fucking legs! Pinch your tits! Hard! Harder! You want me to stop and do it?"

Will ground his teeth and did as he was told and sent sparks of pain shooting through his own chest. Above him, Marcus moved so he was standing right on top of him as Will bent backward. "Good boy ... now grab your cock, boy, grab it and see why you'll never be a real man...."

Will reached for his cock as he was told and watched as Marcus worked the machine into a climax. Fat, thick gobs of white cum splattered across Will's chest, some hitting his neck, and some hitting his taut belly. Marcus continued to work his huge dick, shaking more of his cum all over the kneeling younger man. Then he reached out, grabbed Will by the hair again, and pulled him forward.

And wiped his dick off in that curly black hair.

"Hey, bravo, boss!" A new voice in the room surprised both men, and Marcus turned away to look at him.

"I didn't even hear you come in, Frank," Marcus said, tucking his slightly depleted machine away.

"Yeah, well, you were busy." Frank Dobbs grinned, and it wasn't a pretty sight. All the workouts in the world couldn't change the fact that he was ugly to the bone, a big man with a face that could prevent trucks from starting, let alone stop them in action. He was wearing sweats and a loose tank top that showed off his built-up chest and upper arms, and a weightlifter's belt was draped over one shoulder.

"What do you want, Frank?" Marcus asked.

"I just wanted to let you know that the Hong kid split town. You want I should send the tape?"

"Of course. No harm in letting people know I mean business. Yes, send it at once, by messenger. To the family, and to the business in Queens. And then to the distributor. Anything else?"

"Nah. But we're gonna need a new helper. And you told me to remind you that you got a private session with that model today."

Marcus nodded. "Oh yes ... well, that takes care of me for the afternoon. You want this piece of shit?" He pointed down at Will, who was still on his knees, the cum drying on his chest and belly, his head hung low.

"Sure thing, boss!"

"Well, I got his mouth, why don't you plug his butt? Take your time, I'll put out the 'Help Wanted' sign. And do me a favor—he was kind of slow to respond today. Teach him not to be."

Frank pulled the weightlifter's belt off his shoulder and doubled it in his hands. "You got it, boss. My fuckin' pleasure."

"Of course it is." Marcus left as Frank advanced.

Two hours later, Frank left the private workout room, swinging the belt around and whistling. An hour after that, Will Rodriguez left the gym, and grimly passed a bright sign in the window advertising that a job opening was available.

CHAPTER ONE

CHAPTER ONE

I.

The cab left him off at 7th Avenue and Christopher Street, and Tom recognized the corner from pictures he had seen. It was early evening, still light out, but the workday was done and the streets seemed full of all sorts of people. He stepped out, dragging his heavy duffel bag after him and swinging the lighter knapsack over one shoulder. It had been a luxury, taking the cab from the Port Authority, but he would have plenty of time to explore the subways later. Now, with everything he owned in the world crammed into two pieces of luggage, he would go directly to the address given him over the phone and check out his first apartment.

Tom Kake was almost twenty-one years old, a

compact midwestern blond. Corn-fed, his friends had liked to joke back at school. With his blue eyes and clean-shaven good looks, he had been the stereotypical all-American kid, right out of some tiny town in the middle of nowhere, right off the fuckin' farm, for crissakes, with the shit on his boots to prove it.

As he walked, he tried not to act too much like a tourist. It was very difficult. This is it, he screamed to himself as he walked, a crumpled-up piece of paper in one hand. New York City! The Village! This is where it all happens! And I'm gonna live here! He passed a bar with an open door, and the sounds of country western music reached his ears. Three men were standing on the steps outside the front door, and two of them gave Tom looks of such frank appraisal that he almost blushed. As he passed by, one of them laughed.

Oh, jeeze, Tom thought, his ears reddening. I am such a rube. I probably look like I got hay sticking out behind my ears. Trying to act nonchalant and knowledgeable, he crossed the street and looked casually into several store windows. Clothing and jewelry seemed to dominate what he saw, or at least that's what he thought most of that stuff was. One window held him mesmerized for a moment; could those things in it be what they looked like? He glanced up to find a man looking back at him from the doorway of the shop, his eyes shadowed under the brim of a black leather motorcycle cap, his bare chest furry and tanned under a black leather vest. And what was that silver glint on his chest? Tom blinked and then his blush faded into pale surprise as he real-

16

ized that the man had one nipple pierced and was wearing a ring through it.

Welcome to The Village, said a little voice in Tom's brain. He managed to smile, and then continued to walk on, trying to look in other windows, but not too closely. Two blocks away, he finally regained his composure enough to laugh at himself.

"I do have hay sticking out of my ears," he said out loud, startling only one or two passersby. "I just have to get over it!"

"Yeah, get over it, Mary," echoed a young man in a tight white T-shirt. He had piercings too, although Tom gratefully noticed that they were through the boy's ears and ... nose? "That's the attitude."

Tom laughed again, tried not to stare at the ring in the young fellow's nose, and heaved his duffel bag down. "Excuse me, but could you help me find someplace?"

The youth grinned and laced his thumbs through the belt loops in his jeans. "Depends on what kind of place, hon."

"Uh ... this is the address." Tom showed his piece of paper and the youth studied it thoughtfully.

"I think you're on the wrong side of town, mister. That's an east side address."

"What?" Tom looked at it, as though it would tell him something he hadn't seen before. "But the landlord said it was in The Village!"

"Well yeah, the East Village, maybe, although I think it's kind of on the edge of that, y'know?"

"Oh." Tom took the paper back. "Uh ... is it far to walk?"

With the help of the young man in the white T-shirt, Tom ended up having his first ride on the subway anyway, and emerged in a neighborhood much unlike what he had just left. In the cool of the evening, vacant lots were filling with people playing radios, motorcycles raced up and down the streets, and kids dodged traffic, shouting at each other. He showed the paper to several more people, and was answered with shrugs, answers in halting English, and in one case, a language that sounded like Russian. Finally, he discovered the building and rang the bell for the super.

An hour later, he stood in the center of a one-room catastrophe, with peeling wallpaper and a pockmarked floor, and a bathroom that had more rust in it then viable porcelain. One window was boarded up; the other was so grimy he could barely see through it. There was a bed with a thin, stained mattress on it, two wooden chairs, and an old formica-covered kitchen table with several long ridges dug into it.

"This is a 'furnished, sunny studio, convenient to city nightlife and transportation' and all the rest of that stuff?" Tom asked, as the super handed over a key.

"Yep. Dat's furnishing," the man indicated the bed, chairs and table, "and the sun comes in da window in da morning. An' ya can hear da nightlife startin' up now, can't ya?"

Indeed, the sounds of various musics were coming from all directions, including, Tom thought morosely, through the walls.

"I'm havin' the glass guy in dis week ta replace da missing window. It's hot enough so's ya won't catch cold 'r nuthin'. Y'said you got no kids, so we

18

won't put th' kiddie bars, an' you can sit on th' window ledge if you gets too hot, y'know?" He turned the faucet on in the "kitchen" sink and water flowed out, slightly brown looking at first. "Ya got new pipes in 'ere, should have no problem widda sink or nuthin'. Terlet works. You bring in a air conditioner, an' we charge ya fer the extra 'lectricity. No charge fer fans. Ya want da blankets an' stuff?" The man idly scratched under one arm. "Dey bin washed since da last guy," he added helpfully.

"Yeah, I guess." Tom dropped the duffel bag on the floor. He would have to stay here for a while, at least until he got a decent job and could afford to move. The deposit and two months' rent he had paid for this dump had taken almost all the money he had.

The blankets and a set of worn, light green sheets were delivered, along with a coffeepot and an old fan that the super (Mr. Alfonse D'Angelo, as he introduced himself) said he had in storage. Tom thanked him and sat on one of the wooden chairs, looking at his less-then-glamorous surroundings. When he finally got up to make up the bed, he noticed that the sheets bore an imprint from a hospital, and he collapsed in laughter.

The apartment was just too depressing to stay in. So he changed his shirt and slipped on a light jacket and went out. The streets were full now, and cruising cars slowed down along the stretch of the avenue to reveal young men calling to people walking the pavements. On the corner was a kind of small market or deli, with strange smells of cooked food coming from it, and a cluster of

19

older men sitting out front, listening to a small radio and playing dominoes.

A line of motorcycles stood parked on one block, and Tom spotted a mural featuring the colors of an infamous motorcycle club on the side of one building. A woman wearing a shawl and bright earrings sat on a stoop, the gaudy sign above her advertising five-dollar palm readings.

You wanted a colorful neighborhood, Tom, the young man said to himself. And you got one. It's just a different color then what you had in mind!

He passed a small gym with a neatly painted and lit sign over it, and noted that it was within easy walking distance from his new apartment. Scott, ruggedly good lucking Scott, had been into bodybuilding, and Tom remembered Scott's body fondly. Tom was no stranger to a gym himself, but that was mostly to keep in shape, not to build himself up. It would be nice to have a local gym to belong to. There was a "closed" sign on the door, but there were lights on inside. There was also a help-wanted sign in the window, which he filed away in his memory along with the business hours.

Two young women in motorcycle jackets, with tightly-cropped hair and as many piercings as the young man from Christopher street passed him, holding hands. He was watching a tall woman in tight hot-pants standing at a corner when he suddenly realized that "she" was a man. A convertible with three men in it pulled up to the curb and the "woman" sashayed over to talk to them. Tom, who was just thinking of himself as a suave urbanite, stood in shock, unable to even take his eyes off the scene.

"Not the kind of girl you'd take home to mom, huh?" said a voice next to him.

Tom turned to see a darkly handsome young man wearing a thin gold chain around his neck.

"Uh, no, I guess not."

"Well, she's got to earn a living, just like the rest of us!"

Tom nodded. "Right."

"Care for some company tonight?"

Tom was startled by the question, and looked again at the speaker. He was young, probably still in his late teens. He was wearing a loose, button-down shirt, with the buttons opened down to his belly. His jeans were slung low on his hips, and he had one hand raised. His fingers were rubbing together very slowly.

"I would," Tom started to say, "but ..."

"Hey. Twenty, you'll get my shank for b.j., fifty and I'll give you a nice ride."

Tom felt the need rise in him so strongly that he knew his zipper would break in another minute. He had never met a hustler before, but had fantasized so many times about it. And from the look of the young man, he would give a nice ride indeed.

"But I can't," Tom reluctantly admitted. "No cash. Sorry."

"Hey, no problemo, man. Have a nice night." The hustler casually walked away.

Tom wandered through the neighborhood for another hour, watching it pulse with life. It was definitely not The Village of his dreams, but it was not without its queer component. He spotted a few more transvestite hookers, and several more hustlers as well as a complement of real

21

women who plied the same trade. And there were clubs nearby, with people in black leather slinking in and out and kids of all kinds dancing and cruising and drinking and puking. He got offers of sex, drugs, and more sex, and when he finally went back to his brand new "sunny loft," he was caught between depression and lust.

Tom Kake had only had one boyfriend, and that was back at college. And college was over now, no degree, but it hadn't been the right place for him, so he left to seek his fortune on his own. The disappointment in his mother's voice over the phone and the resignation in his father's when he had asked for a loan had been bitter, but not as bitter as the parting from Scott.

Scott had been older, wiser, more experienced. He had also been from a town as small as Tom's had been, but he was "out." Everyone back home knew he was gay. Tom admired Scott for being that way, but never dared to try and tell his family. How could he? His father would probably throw up, and then disown him, and his mother would get that long-suffering look of terrible sadness, yet another thing gone wrong in her terrible life. And in his small town, soon everyone would know, the way everyone in *his* town knew about Scott. Well, maybe Scott could laugh at being "town faggot," but Tom couldn't. And yet, when Scott graduated and moved to San Francisco, Tom had contemplated going with him.

"What, are you out of your mind, Tommy?" Scott had asked, even as he was packing. "A closet case like you, off to fairyland? Get real, pal. When I get out there, I'm going totally out, brother, get out of my way. Gonna join queer groups and go to queer clubs and march in queer parades, the whole nine yards."

"Jeeze, c'mon, Scott, you don't mean that! You'd be on TV sooner or later, and then everyone will know...." Tom was sitting crosslegged on Scott's bed, watching him pack.

"That's the point, kiddo. No more closets in my life, except to hang my queer clothes in." He slammed the lid of one suitcase closed and pressed down to seal it.

"You know I hate that word," said Tom sullenly.

"Yeah, you do. But that's too bad, Tommy, 'cause that's what you are. Gay as a jay, queer as a three-dollar bill." Scott threw the words like punches, making Tom lower his head to get away from them. "You're a nice, queer cocksucker, my friend, whether you like the words or not. And if you wanna stay hidden for the rest of your life, y'all better find some dumb girl to marry and force yourself to get it up and give her a few brats. Then, you can move back home and raise fucking soybeans and brats for the rest of your fucking life. Who knows, maybe you can hire some guy to help out and maybe get him to fuck you now and again." He picked up another case and began loading it. "But I don't call that living."

"Scott, don't be angry, man, I mean, we're probably never gonna see each other again!"

Scott drew himself up and looked evenly at his younger friend. "Yeah, well, especially if you do go back to Ass Scratch, Indiana, and live in a nice four-bedroom closet."

Tom shot up and headed for the door. "Well, fine, go off to your fairyland and see if I give one big shit!"

Scott laughed and grabbed hold of Tom as he was trying to pass by, and drew him into a violent embrace, forcing his mouth down on Tom's, and kissing him deeply. It worked its usual magic, and Tom melted in Scott's arms as Scott ran his hands over Tom's back and ass, and then brushed over his crotch, never stopping the kiss.

Tom rose to the occasion, as he always did, and Scott moved his mouth over Tom's face, kissing his cheeks and eyelids, and sweeping across to gently bite his earlobe. Tom groaned and pressed eagerly into Scott's hand, and began to move his own hand toward Scott's belt. Abruptly, Scott pulled away. Tom opened his eyes in surprise.

"Yeah, you give a shit," Scott said, closing his second suitcase. "I'm sorry we had to fight on our last day together, but I think you're right, Tommy. We're probably never gonna see each other again. But if you ever get tired of living a lie, come out West and look me up."

Tom lasted exactly six months without his friend and lover before the atmosphere at the school made him claustrophobic. That was when he called his parents and told them he was going to New York. He also told them some stuff about having a job and an apartment waiting, could they just give him enough for the deposit and moving expenses? And they had.

And now he was here. When he turned the light on, New York's most populous residents scurried away, but he was too tired to care. The vision of that first hustler blended with his warm memories of Scott, and he kicked off his shoes, thinking of Scott's long dick, the smell and taste of it. He set the fan on one of his chairs and positioned it so it would catch the breeze coming in through the cracks in the boards covering one window, and thought again about the young hustler. By the time he lay down on his institutional sheets, his own dick was hard, curving up from his body in the strange way it did, rising from the nest of blond pubic hair.

He worked his hand up and down, thinking of the movement of the hustler's hips: I'll give you a good ride, his fantasy image said. Groaning, he turned over on his side, leaving his naked ass up to catch the light breeze coming via the fan. He could just imagine Scott's hands parting his ass cheeks, the cool feeling of the lube being pressed into him, and the slow feeling of fullness as Scott lowered his dick into Tom's tight asshole and began to gently pump. Oh, it was so nice when Scott fucked him!

Tom's hand worked his dick even harder as he imagined what the dick on that young hustler would look like. It would be not too long, but fat, he decided. Really fat, with a foreskin. (Tom had only seen pictures of men with foreskins. All his friends and the boys he watched in the showers were cut.)

Tom imagined sucking on that hustler's thick, uncut meat while Scott slowly fucked him from behind. The thought of two dicks at once made him shudder in pre-orgasmic agony, and he turned back onto his back to shoot his wad straight up in the air, a strangled cry coming from his lips.

He let it dry where it fell and fell asleep right away, to the sounds of salsa coming from the apartment next door.

CHAPTER TWO

II.

Ronald A. Marcus was the undisputed king of his world. It was a small kind of world, and he knew it, but the size was never an issue to him, at least when it came to domains. It was the degree of power he had over his subjects and ministers which was his main concern.

As a young man, Marcus had discovered a god. It had been a rather quiet revelation, borne to him on the back covers of comic books rather then by burning bushes and similar visitations. But where other young men read the prophecies and shrugged, or dallied half-heartedly with false gods and simple answers, Marcus threw himself into his new religion with a passion that would outstrip all others until much later in his life.

"Impress Your Friends!" was one goal of his, promised by the glamorous advertising. For during his early life, there was little that was impressive about Ron Markoski. Skinny, pale, uninspired by either books or music and uninterested in organized sports, Ron had worried his parents. But they had four other worries, two older and two younger, and if one out of five wasn't destined to be a star, well, life would go on. Let the eldest son go out for football (like his old man), and let the youngest daughter win a state scholarship. The second child, another girl, was pretty and popular, and the baby boy, Ron's little brother, played the piano, was a Little League all star, and became an Eagle Scout. Ron? Well, Ron's mother used to say firmly, Ron's a *good* boy.

A bland, uninteresting, unimpressive *good* boy, lost in the middle of a family, neither terribly talented nor terribly popular. Until the revelation, he had been barely interested in himself as well, content to allow his siblings to claim their assorted glories, and more interested in reading comics then doing almost anything else. He would daydream about being a super-hero, strong and invincible, crushing bad guys left and right and saving ... well, saving someone. At the age of his revelation, Ron already knew that he had little interest in saving blonde-haired *girls* in skimpy costumes. But he tried his best not to think about it: When he did, it was bitter irony to him that the only thing interesting about him was that he was a faggot.

"Learn Confidence! Walk Proud!" These were two other prophecies that sounded good when he read them. For surely he would have to learn how to be confident. Every time he tried to stand up to someone (especially his older brother) he got squashed like a bug. And he would like to walk proud, if only he had something to be proud of.

He wrote for the book in the advertisement, and showed pictures of the equipment necessary to his father when winter came around. Dad's eyes had raised in skeptical amazement, but when Elder Son, the football player, also mentioned that such equipment would come in handy for him as well, Dad relented and under the tree that year was a brand new weight set, with a bench and more books, and a pair of gloves for each boy. It was placed in their room, between their beds, with strong hints that fighting over it would result in it being placed in the garage.

Ron kept the ad from the back of the comic book in a drawer by his bed, and looked at it often. Impressing friends, gaining confidence, building a spectacular body, and beating the crap out of any beach-side bully who kicked sand in his face were his earliest goals. But as his older brother stopped showing off and began slacking off, and high school gave way to college (which meant that Ron got the bed by the window and little brother moved in), it was Ron who slavishly continued to work out. Every day, without fail, he returned to the bench and lifted the weights that the books told him to, in the ways that they showed.

He watched programs on TV that had muscular men in tight clothing doing exercises designed for specific purposes. Want a washboard stomach, rippling with power? Do this! Want big upper arms, a massive chest, leonine shoulders? Do this!

31

He subscribed to special magazines and altered his diet, and started running every morning before school.

And, oh, did they notice! At first, almost everyone laughed. Little, skinny, pale and uninteresting Ron Markoski, trying to be a bodybuilder? Who did he think he was? But his mother agreeably cooked the new foods he suddenly wanted, and added raw eggs to milk shakes for him, and began to start comparing his dedication and progress with his siblings. He cared about his health, she often noted. And he ate only good, healthy things, and was very responsible for a boy his age.

His early morning runs began to work on his endurance, and the daily exposure to wind and sun began to add color to his face and arms and legs. When he went to high school, he took swimming and weight lifting courses, already way ahead of many boys in his class. For by now, his skinny body had vanished. Or rather, it had blossomed. He was already tall, destined to be the tallest boy in his class when he graduated. But his shoulders were broad, his waist firm and narrow, and he could lift his two younger siblings, one under each arm, with such ease that it astounded folks who saw it.

He was impressing people, and Ron liked that, but he still lacked real friends. He seemed painfully shy around girls, which made him even more attractive to them. Weight lifting and bodybuilding were solitary sports to him, and even when he began to work out at school, he never seemed to be able to form the relationships with his fellow classmates that he saw other people having. He did know several things though. One, his body was becoming truly beautiful. Perhaps it was in his genes that he could look so good and build himself so well, but what he saw in the mirror was damn close to the ideal bodies he saw in the magazines he had. And two, he was big. Not only in muscles, but in what hung between his legs. He compared himself to the other boys in the locker rooms and felt very pleased. But until his senior year, he was still very much a virgin.

His coach saw great things in Ron's future, and advised him to compete in local, then state, and then regional competitions for boys his age. Coach also warned him away from those drugs of choice for body builders, steroids, with the simple statement that continued use of them would eventually shrink his manhood. Ron immediately tossed away the bottles he had furtively purchased from a local sleazoid, and made a mental note to beat the shit out of him if he ever saw him again.

He won his school's gym medals so easily that they weren't worth bragging about. Soon he was traveling to other districts, other towns, and then cities, and then other states. These things started out small, but rapidly became the biggest part of Ron's social life. He worked part time to finance his trips out of town, and his Dad gave him a used car so he wouldn't have to do all his traveling by bus. And he began to win. Trophies and medals hung from his bedroom walls in no time; and at last, there was something *really* interesting about Ron. His parents talked about him, and showed their friends pictures of their middle child, tan and handsome, and holding some prize or another. And it was on the show circuit that

Ron finally saw where his dedication to building his form could lead. It was at a state final where he lost his virginity, not once, but twice, during a wild after-show celebration.

It happened almost like a dream. Ron had left the stage, holding the garish trophy and wearing a gold medallion, his eyes dazed by the flashbulbs and the looks of pride that his parents were giving him. He had a room at a local motel. There would be photo shoots the next day, and Mom and Dad were returning home that night. Covered in kisses and almost worn out from all the smiling and hand-shaking, he had retired to his room only to find that several other competitors had a party waiting for him, with kegs and girls and very little clothing on anyone.

Oh, how they partied! The other young men seemed genuinely glad that Ron had won, that he would go on to the regional contests and represent their state. They thought he could win big time, and he glowed with their praise and the excitement of their admiration. This was what he really wanted, not the simpering admiration of weak little girls, but the manly respect of men; strong, attractive men. He drank more then he should have and danced a lot, in a mix of male and female bodies that often made it difficult to tell who was dancing with who. Firm pecs and masculine shoulders bounced and shook on all sides of him, and he drank more and more to keep his own feelings in check. Of course, it had the opposite result.

At one point late in the party, the most beautiful girl there came on to him by simply sliding one hand into his pants and grasping the hardness she had spotted during the dancing. He yelped his astonishment, and she moved in closer and shouted, "I want you to fuck me!"

The whole room heard, and approved! Before he knew it, Ron was having his pants almost torn off him, revealing (for the first time publicly) what Will Rodriguez would someday call his 'machine.' Girls "ooohhhed," and some of the guys gasped, but his bold partner was undaunted. She flung herself back on the bed, and Ron found himself propelled toward her and into her by a crush of willing hands.

She shrieked when he entered her, and he felt her welcoming him into her and gasped himself. For a moment, he didn't know what to do, but instincts took over, and his hips began to pump. He heard hoarse, manly cheers behind him, and in response to them, made his hip movements more powerful. There, that was better! He closed his eyes, so he wouldn't have to look at her twisted, screeching face, and pumped, and thrust, feeling the warmth and the softness and driving forward.

"Do it, man, do it, do it!"

"Fuck 'er! Fuck that bitch!"

"Give 'er one for me!"

Their encouragement rang in his ears, driving him faster and harder, until her excited screams became startled gasps, and he knew that whatever girls did when they came, she was doing it. He felt her tighten around him, her legs flying up to grasp him around the waist and pull him in, and the sudden movement made him cry out. He opened his eyes to watch her. But she was oblivious to him, thrashing around and crying out to God.

Another young bodybuilder couldn't stand it any more and climbed on the bed naked, his own cock aimed at her lips. As she opened her mouth to scream again, he thrust neatly past her lips and down her throat.

Ron felt a tremor of pleasure pass through him as he saw this. *Yeah*, he thought, violently screwing his machine into the squirming (but now more silent) girl. *That's it, take it, you hungry bitch, take my meat, take another one down your slutty mouth.* He felt an orgasm building, and suddenly saw pricks, lots of pricks, entering his field of vision. The audience to this spectacular fuck were also joining in, hands busily working on rampant dicks; and as thick, white manjuice began to splatter the girl's body and face, Ron exploded into her soaking wet cunt. It was fast, so fast he felt cheated, and he violently pushed himself at her several more times to get what little pleasure he could out of spite. When he pulled out of her, he shouted, "Who's next?" and was elbowed aside as someone came to take his place.

Ron walked away, found his pants, and pulled them on, disgusted with himself. He left the room, even though it was his room, and stood out in the hall, taking deep breaths, as though he had breathed tainted air.

If that was sex, he wanted no part of it! Slapping his big cock into some screaming, sticky girl, using the body he worked so hard on to make her even more senseless? What was the good in that? Jerking off seemed a lot more fun, compared to what had just happened. He looked up to see that he had been followed by another young man, dressed only in a pair of shorts.

"Great fuck," the other boy said. He brushed some brown hair out of his eyes.

"Yeah," Ron answered.

"Listen—I know you gotta shoot tomorrow morning. Ain't no way you're gonna get those cowboys outa your room if you wanna sleep. Wanna crash in my room?"

The boy (his name was Vic) took him to another room, where it was mercifully quiet. Ron took a shower to get the smell of the cigarette smoke out of his hair and the feel of that girl (whose name he never knew) off of his body. When he stepped out of the shower, Vic was there, with a towel, and Ron silently let the boy dry him. Vic hadn't been in the competition—he had come to watch—but he was clearly a beginner bodybuilder. He had lost the adolescent softness and was already building a good set of shoulders. He looked about eighteen years old, maybe a young nineteen.

They didn't speak, and Ron didn't say anything when Vic carefully handled his cock and balls, and then dried his legs, while kneeling in the small bathroom. Ron's cock grew again, knowing what it wanted, and when Vic dropped the towel and lowered his head, Ron grasped hold of his machine and began to stroke it.

"Can I ... can I suck your cock?" Vic's voice was so low, Ron could barely hear the question. But it did register, and before he knew what he was doing, Ron took his free hand and grasped a handful of Vic's hair and turned his face up. He guided his cock into the boy's mouth, just the head, and saw how difficult it would be for the boy to take it all. But the excitement in his eyes made Ron's cock even stiffer, and when Vic began to lash his tongue happily against the soft under-side of Ron's cock-head, Ron sighed.

Oh yeah, this felt right.

Slowly, Ron worked more and more of his mas-sive dick into the willing boy's mouth, keeping his tight hold on his handful of hair. From time to time, Vic would gasp for breath, and Ron would pull out a little, but each time that happened, he would pull on Vic's hair and make the boy wince. Vic made no attempt to get away, only worked harder to open his mouth and throat. He reached up and caressed Ron's low-hanging balls, and arched his head back to take as much of the cock as he could.

In the full-length mirror, Ron could see the attractive couple they made. It was right, so right! He was so tall and powerful, and here was this man, a neophyte in his religion, doing what would come naturally, and worshiping that which was greater. Would he sacrifice for me, Ron won-dered as he began to press his cock into Vic's throat. Will you take it all for me?

He pulled all the way back, until only the head was in Vic's mouth, and then slammed, with all his force, into the back of Vic's throat. Vic made a choking sound, and gagged, but it felt so damn good! The tightness around his dickhead was exquisitely pleasurable, and the sight of the now struggling young man impaled on his big dick was just ecstasy! He pulled back to give the young man a breath and did it again, and again, battering his throat, until a torrent of fresh, hot cum began to shoot deep in Vic's throat! Yes, this was power!

Ron pulled back again, his dick still pulsating

and pumping out cum, and he bathed the inside of Vic's mouth with it, and then pulled back to splatter the last drops on his face. With tears streaming down his face, Vic took this bath eagerly, gasping for breath even as he licked up this offering.

Ron wiped his dick across Vic's face and told him to clean him up, and then asked if the kid had any Vaseline around.

That had been years and years ago. Now, Ron Marcus (such a more powerful sounding name, much better for competition) owned his own gym, sold two successful bodybuilding tapes and one book, and had a whole wall full of medals and trophies and photos with stars. He had lots of money in the bank, but he still came to "work" at his own little storefront gym, mostly because he was a much-sought-after trainer. In interviews, he often explained that if he hadn't had access to great trainers in his youth, he wouldn't be where he was, and now, it was payback time. He would make himself available to ordinary city youths who wanted to break out of poverty and drug abuse. He would teach them to be healthy and disciplined and give them another way to look at life. The mayor even gave him an award for this work, and it hung in his office right where he could see it.

"Yeah, life is good, isn't it, shithead?" Marcus asked rhetorically. For the only other person in his office with him as he recalled the pleasures of his youth was one of the latest in a long line of cocksuckers whom Marcus used and abused with impunity. The man on his knees was gagged by as much of the machine as could fit (uncomfortably) in his mouth and throat, and could only renew his weak efforts to breathe around the massive obstruction.

A knock sounded, and Marcus hit a button on his desk. Frank walked in, and his ugly face twisted into a smile when he saw what was going on.

"Job applicant, boss," he said poking a thumb behind him. "He's in the outer office. Name's Tom. Cute ass. New in town." He stressed the last line suggestively and laughed. "Real chicken. Wanna see him?"

Marcus pulled the cocksucker off his dick, and the man leaned forward, gasping for breath. "Get out," was the owner's curt command, and the man hurriedly did so, edging past the grinning Frank without raising his eyes. As Frank laughed louder, Marcus hit a button on his desk and the video monitor mounted on the wall came to life, displaying a blond-haired youth in the outer office, studying the awards and trophies displayed there.

"Let me see his application."

Marcus scanned the sheet, reading out loud to himself. "Hm. Twenty-one next month. No degree, some college. Come to us from nowhere, Alabama. Lives ... what, three blocks away?" He looked up. "So? Is he queer?"

Frank nodded. "Oh yeah."

"Pity. I like breaking the straight boys." Marcus looked at the screen again, and then stood up, his robe open around his magnificent body. His machine was still hard. "Let me get dressed, and I'll talk to him."

Tom's face lit up the first time he saw Mr. Marcus. The pictures on the wall in the outer office just didn't do this man justice!

Ron Marcus was not just a big man, he was huge. Clad in sweatpants and a tight T-shirt, his broad chest and massive upper arms seemed to be on display. He walked forward with a strong, direct confidence, his dark brown hair closely cropped around an expressive, proud head. His eyes were an intense, icy dark gray, and Tom did indeed have to look up to meet them. Marcus' grip was firm, but brief, and when he swept one arm out to indicate a chair in the office, Tom was only too eager to sit down.

His knees were already weak.

"Pleased to meet you, Tom," Marcus said, putting the folder with the job application down on the desk. "Ever have any experience working in a gym? Or working out in one?"

"Well, no, I never worked in one, but I used to work out a little at school," Tom replied. "Never, um, professionally, but you know, to keep in shape."

"Nothing wrong with that!" Marcus glanced at the file again. "Most of the men who come here just want to keep their bodies fit. But you're still young—you know it's not too late to start a building program if you want one."

"I'd love to!" Tom admitted. "But first, I have to get a job."

"Right ... well, here's the job in a nutshell. We call you the maintenance manager, but you're really a combination janitor and towel boy." Marcus grinned, and Tom suddenly felt like a wolf had bared its teeth at him. He was glad he was sitting, and laughed weakly.

"It's not glamorous work. You're here a lot. You wash the floors and walls, clean out the pools,

41

disinfect everything, and handle the laundry collection for our service. You keep the machines in the locker rooms stocked, hang up the mats and keep the private rooms spotless. In return, you get the lowest level membership, and of course, your salary." Marcus mentioned a number that seemed awfully low, and then looked intensely at Tom, whose eyes suddenly lost some of their shine.

"I know it's not a lot. But you do get full medical benefits and a gym membership with it." He shrugged. "And you never know what else. If you're serious about building up, we can arrange some private training sessions from time to time. And there are some other opportunities here as well. A lot of the men who come here are always looking for part time help, or need bodies for short term jobs. What do you think?"

"It sounds interesting, Mr. Marcus, but, well, I was hoping for a little more money. It seems awfully expensive to live in New York."

"That's right, you just moved here! What do you think of the big city?"

"It's sure big!" Tom laughed again. "It's so crowded! And the prices are so high ... but I've always wanted to live here. *Everything* happens in the city."

"Ah! Small-town boy, huh?" Marcus leaned back, his arms hooked across the back of his chair, pulling his shirt tighter across his chest.

"Yeah," Tom said, trying not to blush. He could barely take his eyes off the gym owner's chest! He tried to keep himself controlled, and had the awful thought that he'd lick his lips. "I went to college...."

"Yes, I saw that. But no degree yet."

"No. I wanted to work." Tom had practiced that answer so that it came out smoothly. Marcus nodded.

"Well, I can understand that. But you'll find it harder to get a decent job without that paper, my boy. Did you like college? Have a lot of friends there?"

"Sure, it was OK."

"Anyone special?"

Tom started to nod, even as he realized how odd the question was. He took a deep breath and laughed again, trying to dispel his nervousness.

"You living alone here in the big city, or did you come here with a friend?" Marcus asked, his eyes boring into Tom.

"Uh ... I live alone," Tom stammered.

"Tough to be on your own in a new town, Tom," Marcus said, his deep voice suddenly silky. "You should make some new friends." He lowered one arm and absently adjusted himself between the legs, the movement noticeable, but the result hidden by the desk. This time, Tom did blush, and he reached up to brush some hair out of his eyes. Any excuse to look away!

"Oh, I will, Mr. Marcus. I expect I will...." he said. "Um ... I'll need more time to think about this. When did you want someone to start?"

"Immediately," Marcus said, leaning forward. "But I'll give you a day or two. In fact, I'll give you until Friday. If you say yes ... and Tom, I want you to say yes ... you can start on Monday."

"OK. I'll, uh, call you as soon as I make up my mind," Tom said, his words falling over each other. His cock was hard between his legs, and his knees were still weak, but he managed to rise.

43

"Make it quick, Tom. If someone else comes in between now and then, I'll have to make a decision, whether you have or not." Marcus rose, too, and stretched out a hand, and Tom shook it. This time, Marcus' grip was firmer, and he held Tom's hand captive even longer. "Listen ... before you leave, you'll want a tour. Come with me."

Tom felt the weight of the man's commanding voice, and any half-hearted objections died in his throat. He followed Marcus out of the office and through the waiting room, and then into the corridors of the gym. Well-remembered sounds of weight machines and the smell of bleach and sweat assaulted Tom's ears and nose, and his hard-on tightened against his leg.

"This is the free-weight room," Marcus said, indicating the padded room with the window. Tom saw five free-weight areas set up, and neat racks of weights and bars on one wall. Two men were in there now, one warming up, and the other using what looked like a very heavy bar to do power lifts.

"We've got the latest in machines, too," Marcus said, leading Tom across the hall. This room didn't have a window, but there was a sign on the door that said "Unoccupied." Marcus opened the door and showed off a very state-of-the-art equipment room, with machines that Tom both recognized and was baffled by. Some of them had digital readouts on them, and Marcus walked Tom throughout the room, pointing special ones out.

"And this baby comes from Sweden. It helps define abs, very good for the stomach, very good for the ass. Twenty minutes a day will form up a

44

healthy man. And you've seen these, right? They use tension bands instead of weights. Makes it easier to pick up after a long day, right?" His laughter was strong and hearty, and Tom joined in, amazed at all the expensive machinery here.

"I got the bikes in another room, with the rowing machines, the treadmills, and the stair machines. This stuff is all progressive resistance in here. Want to see the pool?"

Of course, they saw the pool, and the sauna, and the smaller hot-tub—like whirlpools, and the steam room. "We use more water every day then the restaurants on the block," Marcus noted. "And we're much cleaner."

Throughout the facility, there were men working out, or relaxing. The vast locker rooms had private lockers and smaller ones available for renting on a hourly basis. More men were there, with towels around their waists, or in the process of changing. The odor of masculinity was heavy here, and Tom breathed it in like the smell of home cooking.

"And we have private workout rooms for men who belong to the higher levels of membership, the ones who get private training sessions with me or Frank. You met Frank, right?"

Tom nodded, remembering the ugly man. "Well, he's just starting a session with one of our promising boys. Let me introduce you." Marcus steered Tom toward one of the smaller rooms, and knocked. The sign on the door said "occupied," and there was a blue light lit up on a panel next to the sign. The light changed to green, and Marcus turned the handle and opened the door for Tom to enter.

BADBOY BOOKS

The small room had two pieces of equipment in it, plus a rack of accessories, a chair, and a frame set up for stretching exercises and chin-ups. It was very well designed, Tom thought. Just like a home gym would be, except for the mirrors on the walls.

Frank was there, standing, in gray sweats. He was holding a stopwatch, and had a clipboard under one arm. The man on the resistance machine, in contrast to Frank's amazing ugliness, was absolutely beautiful.

He must be Hispanic, Tom thought, watching the young man pushing his legs against the padded bars, stretching the bands to their fullest and then bringing them back slowly. His skin was the color of caramel, his hair long, black, and curly. The three men watched as Will finished his series, and then sat back.

"Good." Frank clicked his watch and noted something on the pad. "It's getting easier to do them within the timeframe. You've been practicing."

Will nodded, wiping the sweat from his forehead.

"Will, this is Tom," Marcus said, coming forward. "He's considering working here."

Will raised a hand, and then he and Tom actually looked at each other. And Tom felt the unmistakable feeling, when their eyes met, that Will liked what he saw as much as Tom liked what he saw! The two men seemed to be of an age, and although Will had a much better body, there was a light masculine grace to Tom as well. They were the same height. Tom knew that they would make a stunning couple, light and dark, slender and built.

46

"Workin' ... here?" Will asked, letting go of Tom's hand.

"Yes," Marcus answered. "To replace Hong."

Will looked away for a moment. "Yeah, well, pleasure to meet you. I gotta get back to work here."

"Right. Sorry to disturb you guys. See you later, Frank!"

Marcus steered Tom out of the room and back to the waiting room, where they met two more men coming into the gym, their bags over their shoulders. Both men greeted Marcus warmly before they went inside.

"Think about it carefully, Tom," Marcus said, laying one hand on Tom's shoulder. "It's not exactly as bad as working at McDonalds, and you do get access to the gym. And like I said, if you need more money, we can talk. Be sure and get back to me as soon as you can; you'll never get another opportunity like this one!" As Tom left the office, he felt a trickle of sweat run down his back. He actually gasped as he exploded out of the gym into the cool air of the street. It was too much! The intense, almost godlike Marcus, the beautiful Will, the atmosphere of a gym, with so many hot men walking around ..!

He took a deep breath and started walking west. He stopped by a street vendor and bought a cold soda, which he tossed back, feeling the coldness and the bubbles wash away his heat and clear his head. As he tossed the can into a trash basket, he knew that he was going to have to buy a newspaper and look for some other jobs.

He just didn't know if he could handle working at the Gold Medal Gym.

47

CHAPTER THREE

III.

"Sorry. We were really looking for someone with more experience."

"Sorry. That position was filled on Monday."

"I'm sorry. But the job requires a degree."

"Hey, sorry, man. But we just can't hire anyone new right now."

"Sorry." "Sorry." "Sorry."

"Sure, we can take you on! Minimum wage for a six-month probation period, with a twenty-five cent raise immediately after that. And you get a free meal every day. Deal?"

Tom looked at the smiling man sitting over the application that was printed on a paper placemat and sighed. "I ... I need to think about it."

The man continued to smile. "Fine, just fine.

Give me a call as soon as you decide, but remember, it's a tough job market out there! I started out as a burger flipper myself, and look where I am now! I'm the assistant manager. In a few years, maybe I can actually start looking into having my own place!" He stood up and walked back behind the counter, leaving Tom to contemplate his cold fries and the newspaper that had so few want ads circled. He did a little mental figuring, and realized that the money he would be paid at this place would leave him less then two hundred dollars a month to live on.

The fries slid into the garishly colored garbage can and fell with a thump, and Tom felt a similar hollow feeling inside himself. He was three days into full-time job-hunting, and two days short of absolute poverty.

When he had left the gym, he immediately bought two newspapers and spent two hours going through the ads and circling the promising ones. Then he found the resume he had prepared back at school and made up a pile of copies, and began his search.

He started out ambitiously, and found that he was just short of a laughingstock with personnel officers. No practical office skills, no serious job experience, no degree, no references, and no snappy clothing were all very funny things to people who often said no to those who had all of the above. He found himself arriving at offices and stores where there were dozens of applicants waiting for interviews for one or two jobs.

He bought macaroni and cheese at the local markets and ate at home, and watched as the few dollars he had left began to trickle away. And each day, he passed the Gold Medal Gym and kept going.

But compared to what he was offered by the fast food place, Ron Marcus' offer was almost princely. And he would get a gym membership with it ... and a chance to meet that cute guy, Will....

"Hey, Blondie!"

He looked up, and then around, and to his surprise, saw Will Rodriguez, leaning against a lamppost. The Hispanic man waved, and Tom felt a lurching shudder that made him feel like he did the first time he ever asked someone to dance. Somehow, he grinned and casually waved back, and then headed over to the man. All nervousness aside, Will's was the first genuinely friendly face he had seen in a long time.

"Hi," Tom said. "What's up?"

"I could ask the same of you, man. You look tired. Still looking for a job?"

"Yeah."

"And it's not going too well, huh? Well, welcome to the new age. I'm kinda surprised, actually. Guys like me are supposed to have lots of trouble finding work, not a guy like you." Will's voice was light, but there was a bite behind them. Tom shook his head, confused.

"What do you mean?"

Will fingered his curly black hair, and then reached over to grab a fingerful of Tom's. "Blond and blue-eyed, you know? Classic American looks. Greasy kids like me, one step out of the barrio, we're not supposed to be hired. Except at McBurgers, or something."

Tom laughed. "But that's where my best offer

came from!" He told Will his job hunting stories, and before he was even halfway through, Will took his arm.

"Put a hold on this, Blondie. If you're gonna give me the whole story, you're gonna do it over breakfast."

Tom glanced at his watch. It was almost 4:00. "Breakfast?"

Will guided Tom to a small restaurant where the man at the door seemed to know him, and they ended up sitting at a booth. Tom's stomach growled, but he fought it, knowing that he would have to tell Will that he wasn't hungry. When the menus arrived, he did just that.

"Relax, Blondie. I got some spare change. Eat some real food for a change, that hungry look ain't good for job hunting."

Tom almost melted with gratitude. The rest of his story slid out while they waited for the food, and before too long, he was telling Will why he'd left school.

Will forked a mouthful of omelette into his mouth and nodded. "That's a bitch, man. But you know, my mom doesn't know about me. I even date a few girls once in a while to keep her happy. The girls like it because I take 'em dancing and we *dance*, and I don't use those old, 'Oh, baby if you *looove* me' lines after we leave. Mom likes it, 'cause she doesn't hear any stories about any bad way I treat the girls. She brags about me, y'know? I never got one knocked up, I'm a good Catholic boy." He laughed, his teeth white and strong.

"I never dated girls. I told my parents that no one interested me locally, and wrote them that I had a girlfriend at college."

54

"Life's a bitch. But it sounds like you had some hot stud at the school, man."

"Yeah." Tom flushed. "He was great."

"Topman, huh?"

Tom nodded, too embarrassed to speak.

"Yeah, me too. Nothin' like fucking. That's what *I* do for a living."

"Huh?"

"I fuck for a living. Guys pay good money to get worked over by this Puerto Rican stud. It's OK, but it's strictly nightwork." He indicated his cup of coffee. "Breakfast in the afternoon, get it?"

"Oh." Tom nodded, his mind awhirl. Will was a prostitute? A hustler? Memories of the various sex workers in his neighborhood and his own frustrated desires for them and what they offered flooded his brain. Will sat there, relaxed and sexy, slowly eating his breakfast and chatting from time to time, and did not look like Tom's idea of a hustler.

For one, Will was just too sensual. The men Tom kept meeting were hot (mostly), but theirs was an urgent heat, one that promised immediate gratification and a rough edge. Will moved like a panther, slow and gracefully, his muscles hinted at, his strength only suggested.

He would take a long time with me, Tom thought suddenly. He would tease a lot, and then make me beg for it....

Under the table, Tom's cock pressed against his fly, and he shifted in his seat. The thought of being pinned under this lithe, dark man was too much, and it brought back the sight of Will on the weight bench, his arms straining, his legs shiny with sweat. It was a few moments before Tom realized that Will was speaking again.

"But it's good you went to college. That's important later."

"Uh, yeah, but only if you finish."

"You can always tell them you finished."

"But what if they check?"

Will shrugged. "Then that's another job you can't have. Sooner or later, you'll find one, and it'll be better then flipping burgers or picking up towels."

"Actually, I was thinking of taking the job at the gym."

Will looked up sharply. "That would be a mistake."

"Why?"

The Puerto Rican man didn't answer at once. He signaled to the waiter for more coffee and poured cream into it before drinking. "Because it's a lousy job, and Marcus won't pay you what it's worth," he finally said. "It's long hours in a hot, sweaty place, and a lot of assholes hang out around gyms. It'd be better to work at Woolworth, man."

"Yeah, but it's the pay plus a membership. And I can walk to work, so I can save on lunch and traveling. I think it'll work, at least for a while. I can always keep looking."

"Yeah, well, you better look harder, pal. The gym is not the place for you. Trust me on this one, OK?" His voice scaled up a little, and he stared at Tom in something that almost felt like anger.

"But ... I really need a job. Now. And that was my best offer...." Tom shrugged helplessly, confused by the man's sudden change of attitude.

"You can get better offers, man. But if you wanna toss your life away at that lousy place, it's your decision. But lemme give you some advice.

Never be alone with Marcus in his office, OK? That's all I gotta say." Abruptly, he stood, draining his coffee, and he waved for the waiter again.

"Wait, Will, don't leave … what did I say?" Tom started to push his chair back.

"No, you stay. Finish eating. I gotta go, OK? I'll see you around." Will snatched the check out of the waiter's hand, tossed a few bills on the table and left before Tom could even say another word. Tom leaned back in his seat, and thought about what just happened and what Will said, and then finished eating.

After he ate, he looked at the list of jobs he had applied for, the number of "no's", the two offers he got, and the amount of money on the table. Will had just paid for lunch with more money then Tom had left.

Taking a quarter from the tip money, Tom called the Gold Medal Gym and told Mr. Marcus that he'd be there on Monday morning.

Monday morning was spent filling out forms and taking a more complete tour of the facilities with a look at what happened behind the scenes. He was introduced to the driver of the laundry truck that came by twice every day, the man from the water cooler company, the guy who filled the juice machine, the exterminator, and the rest of the staff. It wasn't a large staff.

Frank Dobbs was the manager, and he was a huge, ugly man. His nose had been broken at least twice, and his eyes were too close together. He had a habit of smiling when nothing was funny, displaying a twisted mouth filled with yellowed, jagged teeth. But the men at the gym seemed to respect him.

BADBOY BOOKS

There were two part-time floor managers, Alex
and John, who split various shifts between them
and made sure that the rules of the gym were
obeyed. They were both friendly and glad to have
him aboard, since they had been sharing the
duties of the "maintenance man" while waiting
for one to be hired.

And those duties were many! In addition to
being the towel boy, Tom's new job also required
him to mop the place down every night, disinfect
the showers, sauna, locker rooms, and the steam
room, keep the place neat, put equipment back
where it belonged, and keep up with the various
suppliers who serviced the gym. There were a few
vending machines that he had to keep stocked,
one with juices and energy drinks, one with soaps
and shampoos, and one with combs, keychains
and condoms. There was also a glass counter
stocked with vitamins and energy tablets and
other weird stuff, but he was only responsible for
taking orders, not actually stocking it.

"I'm going to be busy," he said out loud, during
his tour.

"Yeah, you sure are," admitted Frank, his teeth
showing. "But you'll get used to it. At first, if you
don't know what the fuck you should do, call me,
or one of the floor guys, or even Mr. Marcus. Get
to know your way around. Just keep this in mind:
Never interrupt a private training session unless
the green light is on, got it? If it's blue, you can
knock. But our boys pay a lot of money for those
sessions, and if you ever interrupt one, you'll be
outa here so fast you'll think you're back in
Kansas, or whatever you came from. Got it?"

"Got it!"

58

Frank grinned, a horrible sight. "Good. I like you, Tommy, you learn fast." He handed Tom two staff T-shirts and a card with a locker number and combination. "This is your locker; you can keep your own gear here if you want. When you're working, always wear the staff shirt. No shoes in the tile areas, only workout boots or sneakers, and don't let me see any of those hundred-dollar sissy running shoes. If you want more stuff with our logo on it, you get a fifty percent discount. Oh ... Mr. Marcus said you might be a little low on cash. Issat true?"

Tom nodded.

"Well, this is an advance on your pay." Amazingly, Frank handed over an envelope as well. "It's coming straight outa your first check, got it? You run off on us before you work long enough to get that check, I'll break your fucking legs, got it?"

"Yeah ... thank Mr. Marcus, OK? This means a lot to me...."

"Yeah well, Mr. Marcus is a whatayoucallit, a humanitarian. He's a real softee sometimes. He'll be around later this week, you can thank him then. In the mean time, let's get you working."

Tom plunged himself into the work wholeheartedly. His strange conversation with Will seemed almost bizarre. How could Will say such things about working at the gym? Sure, as the day went on, Tom realized that he probably was being underpaid for the amount of work he had to do, but it was a job. And Mr. Marcus had even given him a cash advance. Which would come in real handy! Tom was sick and tired of macaroni and cheese dinners.

So he strode around the gym, important in his new shirt, and gathered and delivered towels, and picked up bars and weights and belts, and washed out sinks. At the end of the day, exhausted, he dragged around the huge bucket on wheels and slopped the bleaching disinfectant all over everything.

Then, as the fumes from the disinfectant filled the air, he checked all the rooms and picked up the various items that would make it into the lost and found, and passed by one of the private workout rooms where the light was a steady blue. Without knocking, he continued along his way, picked up his stuff from his locker and said goodnight to Alex, who was closing that night.

Walking home with cash in his pocket, he felt like a new man. A tired man, true, but a new one. He passed the crowd around his neighborhood and felt the comfort of a regular paycheck in his future and smiled at several of the young men who were artfully hanging around his corners.

Soon, he promised himself. Soon, I get what I really need, and then I can work on Will.

But in the meantime, it was the next chapter in his love affair with his right hand.

The second day passed like the first, only he got to know a few of the men who came to the gym. There seemed to be a lot of men who walked through those front doors, but there were also a lot of different levels of membership. Some men came by every day, others a few times a week, others just for private sessions. Some rented their lockers, others used the "free" ones and brought their own locks.

There were some who were just trying to keep in shape and those who were working out in special ways for sports fitness. And then there were the weight lifters and bodybuilders, the men who took their workouts seriously and came to them with the determination of an artist.

So many of them! In all sizes and shapes, big and brawny and small and bandy, swimmers and dancers and truck driver types. And they called to Tom, and he ran to them with towels and shirts and order forms and change, and they grinned at him and showed him their bodies. Their spectacular, sculpted bodies, barely covered in loose, torn tops and skimpy shorts, or in tight, form-fitting lycra that showed off every curve and bulge.

A lot of them were gay, or so it seemed to Tom. A few couples came in together and worked out together, and he liked one couple in particular, a pair of men from the other side of town. Their names were Mike and David, and they seemed to share a secret about their relationship beyond the fact that they were lovers. They greeted Tom warmly, and David was the first to offer him a tip for his services.

Not knowing what to do, Tom tried to return it, but Mike took him aside and explained that this was not only allowed, but in this particular gym, it was encouraged. "We know that Marcus pays you slave wages, kiddo," he said with a wink. "Take it. Buy a beer or something, you need to fill out anyway!"

And Tom did take it, and concentrated on being friendlier to the customers and tried to predict what they might want from him. Despite his getting lost once, forgetting to check the stock on the

shampoo, and leaving one room in a mess because
he hadn't realized that the blue light had finally
gone off, he managed to get a few more tips that
day, and he laughed on his way home that night.
This was going to be easy! Maybe the wages
weren't a lot, but with tips as well ...

Soon! He promised his cock. Soon!

On Wednesday he ran into Will while he was
refilling the soap machine. Will was sharply
dressed, but he had a private locker, and had to
pass Tom to get to it. The Hispanic man paused
for a moment when he saw Tom.

"Well, I guess you took the job," he said simply.

"Um ... uh ..." Tom colored slightly. "I told you,
Will, I really needed ..."

"Hey, congratulations, man!" Will's demeanor
suddenly changed. "I'm glad you got it. But I
gotta get going, you know? Time is money, man."
He strode over to his locker and began to undress.

Tom tried not to peek, tried to remain concentrated on his job, but as Will stripped off his
clothing, Tom felt his long-frustrated dick rise in
impatient fury. Soon! his brain shouted, but his
dick was tired of hearing that. Tom hurriedly
jammed the tiny containers into the machine and
slammed it shut. The noise startled several men
in the locker room, and they turned to see, and
suddenly, half a dozen cocks seemed to turn
toward Tom. He pulled his keys out of the
machine and fled.

In the cool hallway, he panted and tried counting to ten, thinking of bad food and history class,
and anything to get him under control.

Things went from bad to worse after that.

Every man seemed to be making an invitation to him, every bared piece of flesh seemed to want his fingers and his tongue. Every time he turned around, there was another opportunity, another tease, another excuse for his misbehaving dick to stand up and take interest.

Even the sounds of working out seemed to be the sounds of fucking. Every grunt and wheeze, every panting breath and angry cry of effort ... By the end of the day, Tom had to take a long, cold shower.

"I'll never make it," he said out loud as he dressed. He was alone in the locker room. "It's too fucking much!"

But he showed up on Thursday, and as though some capricious entity had heard his prediction, he was faced with his first mechanical catastrophe. In the late afternoon, someone reported that the whirlpool wasn't draining properly. He went downstairs to investigate, and found that this was true, and when he reported it to John, John called a plumber and ordered that the pool room be closed temporarily. Tom would have to come in extra early on Friday to clean and refill the pool. John promised to inform Frank, but somehow, he forgot. No matter, John thought. The door will be open anyway, and no one else should be here.

Tom showed up early, as he was told, and found the door unlocked, which didn't surprise him. He went directly to the pool rooms, and sighed at the mess that the plumber had left. He got his rags and mop, filled a bucket with steaming water, and began his cleanup. There was one nice thing to look forward to. Mr. Marcus, who Tom had seen only once that week, was going to be at the gym today, and he had promised to talk to Tom about designing a workout program for him. It was also payday.

So, he slopped the mop around and cleaned up the area around the pool, and then inside it. Feeling especially diligent, he polished the spouts and water-control levers, and then turned them on to fill it again. The water rushed in, and he gathered his cleaning tools to put them away.

And then he heard a sharp sound. Startled, he let go of the mop, and looked around. There wasn't anyone else in the room with him, and he shook his head. Jeeze, now I'm hearing things, he thought. The place isn't even open yet. But then he heard the sound again.

He turned the water off and listened carefully. There it was again! Sharper now, clearer. And more regular. It was a smacking sound, like a clap. A loud clap. He looked around the room, and followed the sound to a small ventilation grill. Glancing around, the sound now very regular and clear, he realized that the other side of that wall was the small shower room that was used by some of the private-session clients. Walking softly over to the wall, he stood on his toes to try and hear the sound better. He didn't exactly know why it was suddenly so important to be quiet, but he felt it deeply.

Being on his toes barely got the top of his head near the grill. He stood there, listening to the sounds, trying to figure out what to do, when they changed. Now, they were followed by grunts, like the sounds that some men made when they lifted. Smack!

Tom carefully walked away and picked up one of the benches and brought it over to the wall. A twisted feeling in the pit of his stomach made him hesitate again, but he got up on the bench and carefully peered through the grill.

What he saw made him break out in sweat immediately.

Frank Dobbs was in the room, stripped to the waist. He was using what looked like a weight lifter's belt with the buckle removed, to beat the ass and thighs of a man who was face down on the floor in a push-up position. Each swing of the belt caused that heavy slapping sound, and the man on the floor was responding with strangled cries.

The man on the floor was also almost naked. His reddened ass was bisected by a the white bands of a jockstrap. But his beautiful, muscled back and legs were bare.

Despite the horror of the scene, Tom felt aroused. Trying not to make a sound, he carefully cupped his own cock and swallowed hard, watching what was happening.

Frank was relentless. Up and down, the belt swung, cracking sharply against the other man's ass. Sometimes, he shifted his aim, and the belt landed on the man's thighs, and the man would grimace and choke back a protest. But he continued to do his push-ups, his arms pressing his body up and down, driven on by the belt.

It went on and on, until the red began to discolor in some places, and sweat began to pour from the man's body. His grunts became groans, and then honest cries of pain. And while all this was happening, Tom's dick, with a mind of its own, became stiff as his mop handle. The scene was just too intense! The glaring light of the shower room reflecting off the clean tile walls, the stark beauty of the man's body, and the sharp sounds of the brutal beating were almost too *real* to bear. A wave of guilt washed through him, but he maintained a grip on his cock and held his breath, letting it out slowly and quietly. Tom knew somehow that it would mean more than his job if Frank discovered him.

Finally, the poor man on the cold floor dropped onto his chest, awash in his own sweat, his ass and legs heavily bruised from Frank's beating. He covered his head with his powerful arms, as though he expected a blow, and lay there, panting. His entire body shook with exhaustion and pain.

"What the fuck do you think you're doing, you fucking wimp!" Frank's voice was so loud that Tom nearly fell off his bench. He dropped below the grating, his own heart pounding in fear, and listened to the tirade that was beginning.

"I told you one hundred and fucking fifty, you son of a bitch, get the fuck up and get going!"

"I can't! I can't ... not like this...." The man's voice was deeper then Frank's, but it was filled with fear.

A loud whack! sounded, and it wrenched another cry of pain from the man.

"You don't tell me what you can't do, asshole! You just do! Now get that ass up in the air!"

"Frank, please ... I can't...."

"There's that fucking word again! Did I ask if you could, shitface? No!" The whacking sounds continued in a flurry of blows, and Tom slid back up to the grating to watch Frank just swing that belt again and again. The man on the floor cowered and took each blow, trying to keep silent, but each new stripe was accompanied by a desperate, strangled cry of pain.

"You thought you could get out of this by coming in early, didn't you, asshole?" Frank paused and wiped a sheep of sweat from his ugly face.

"I ... I'm sorry, I didn't ... I just wanted to get in an early workout!" The man sounded almost broken.

"Yeah, I believe you. Like I believe the fucking president of the United-fucking-States!"

"Please! Frank, please, I've had enough, I have to get to work...."

"Shut up! You talk too much, asshole. And I am not finished with you." Frank reached into his pocket and took a folding knife out, and Tom froze.

But the ugly man didn't cut or stab his bruised victim. Instead, he cut the straps on the jock, and pulled it off. Then, he bent down by the man's head and made some kind of motion that Tom couldn't see, while saying, "There. That'll keep your fucking mouth busy. Now get your butt up, get those fucking shoulders straight! You don't want to disappoint me, right?!"

As the man struggled to get up into the position Frank wanted, Frank stood up and tugged his gray workout shorts down. Tom stared in helpless fascination.

If the man was ugly from the neck up, his cock was a close runner-up in the ugly competition! But it was big, and it was, Tom noticed, uncut. It rose out of a raggedly hairy crotch, and it was crooked! It actually had a bend to it that looked almost unnatural. Frank lowered a big hand to it and stroked it lovingly, and pulled the foreskin back over the meaty head. It made a bizarre picture, this ugly man with a strong, pumped-up body, slowly bringing his ugly dick to a full erection.

Tom didn't know whether to gag or drool. He stayed absolutely still.

The man on the floor got himself into the position that Frank wanted, his arms holding his body up, his back straight, his ass off the floor. Now, free from the jock, his dick was hanging down toward the cold tiles, and Tom felt a sympathetic shiver.

Frank walked behind the man and kicked his legs wide apart, and the man grunted as he shifted them. Tom realized now that the jockstrap so recently around the man's cock and balls was now in his mouth, and the thought of tasting the sweat and man-essence made him suddenly lightheaded.

"Now hold that position, fucker. You're gonna wait until I get settled, and then you're gonna do that last set of twenty." Frank dropped his shorts to one side, plucking something out of one pocket before chucking them. Tom heard the crinkling sound of a foil package being opened, and watched as Frank unrolled a condom over his thick, twisted cock. Then, Frank lowered himself to his knees and took hold of the man's bruised ass cheeks with both hands. Ignoring the muffled cry of pain, he spread them apart, revealing the wrinkled hole that would house his meat.

"Oh yeah ... gonna take me all the way and come back for more, asshole. Open wide ..."

The man screamed into his gag as Frank abruptly shoved his dick into him. His knees buckled, and his arms gave out, and he fell forward, but Frank relentlessly drove into him. And once Frank was in, a smile broke across his ugly face, and he leaned forward, putting his own muscular arms on the floor on either side of the man he was about to really fuck.

"Get the fuck back up!" he yelled into the man's ear. Frank was now spread over the man, his body held comfortably by his own arms, his dick warmly sheathed in the man's asshole, the feel of those hot, bruised ass cheeks so *goood* against his crotch!

"If you don't want me to fuck you to death, you're gonna get that butt up and make me happy, motherfucker! Do it!"

With herculean effort, the man responded, and Tom saw the incredible. The man rose up to meet Frank's invading organ, and then sank down away from it. And then rose up to be filled again! The man was doing pushups and fucking himself on Frank's twisted dick!

Despite his initial disgust, Tom felt a rising need in himself, and practically tore his cock out of his jeans. It was still hard. He licked his palm and began to stroke it, compelled to watch the scene that was unfolding before his eyes.

The man was amazing! Despite the pain and the humiliation, he continued to rise and drop, and Frank was counting for him.

"That's three, motherfucker, get your ass all the way up, or I'll nail you to the floor like a piece of carpeting! Come on, all the way down, get those chest muscles into it! What are you, some kinda sissy boy? Get the fuck back up here and take my fat dick, asshole! Come on, take it all! That's four! Only sixteen to go, asshole! Think you're gonna make it?"

His cries muffled by the jockstrap in his mouth, the man could only obey, and work his body up and down. Frank seemed to effortlessly hold himself still, accepting the embrace of the man's asshole, and urging him to better performance.

Tom held back a moan as he stroked his own erection. The sights before him were so surreal, he could feel a thick, crooked dick invading his own butthole, and the overwhelming taste of his own sweat and juices on a white cotton jock. He worked his cock with a fury, filled with a desire that had never been a part of him before, and watched as the count went higher and higher.

"That's twelve, fuckface! Only eight more to go! And you better hurry up, 'cause I can't hold out all fucking day, and if I cum before you're finished, I'm gonna finish you on something bigger, got that? Come on, fucker, thirteen, you love it, don't you? Come back for more, asshole, come on back for more of my big dick...."

And the man did, straining and moaning under the gag. And finally, as the numbers crept up, Frank began to meet him halfway, thrusting in time with his push-ups, and then finally, at a cry of "Twenty!", plowing forward with such force that once again, the man was slammed down against the tiles. Frank paid no heed, but shoved and thrust, and then made a hoarse, guttural cry as he spilled his twisted pleasure into the man's tortured butthole.

Tom bit his lip as his own cock spurted, splattering his white cum all over his hand and the wall he was pressed against. It was so hard to keep quiet! But he stayed still, his heart pounding, watching what was happening.

Frank wasted no time lying there and recovering. Instead, he jerked his dick out, making the man twist with sudden pain, and took the condom off it. Laughing, he shook the contents of the scumbag onto the man's head, and then tossed the empty onto his back.

"I'll see you next week, asshole," Frank said, drawing his shorts back on. "And you better be able to do that one-fifty." He picked up a small kit bag by the door and left, laughing, leaving the man shivering on the tiles.

Tom carefully got down from the bench, and sat on it, oblivious to the wetness in his hand and the small trail of cum running down the wall. He finally took a deep breath, and hurriedly pushed his cock back into his pants. He mustn't be discovered! Still reeling over what he had just witnessed, he stood up and looked around the room. He dived for the small pool and turned the water back on to fill it, and pulled a rag out of his bucket. He wiped down the section of wall by the ventilation grille and moved the bench back to where it belonged, and brought the bucket and mop back to their closet. In time, he went back to the room and turned the water off, but he stayed away from the private shower room.

Soon, the day formally started, and people started to come in. Alex was in that day, and Tom told him that the whirlpool was fixed and cleaned, and could he have a break to go get some coffee? Since he had come on so early, Alex let him go, and he rushed out into the cool air.

And ran straight into Mr. Ron Marcus!

Tom looked up in shock and felt his balls shrivel between his legs, but Marcus just smiled down at him. He was big and friendly, and smelled cleanly of mint.

"Good morning, Tom," the man said. "Where are you heading so fast? Don't you want to collect your pay?"

"Uh … I … um, I was just going for some coffee," Tom replied. "Sorry, I wasn't looking where I was going! I'll be back soon."

"Nonsense! Too much caffeine is bad for you; you're already too jumpy. Come into my office, we'll settle up, and you can tell me how you're doing. We were supposed to talk about a training schedule for you today, weren't we?" Without allowing Tom another second to protest, Marcus steered him back through the front door and through the lobby.

"I understand you came in early today to take care of the pool room. That's good. Frank tells me you learn quickly, too. I thought you had the right stuff, Tommy, and I like being right!" Marcus unlocked his door and ushered Tom in. Once inside, he took off his coat and hung it up, and then took a seat at his desk, his massive frame settling into his chair comfortably.

"Thank you, Mr. Marcus," Tom said, genuinely glad that no one had complained about him. But he felt an odd sensation in the pit of his stomach at the sound of Frank's name, and he struggled to keep his face free of expression. He hadn't even had time to think about what he witnessed that morning, and here he was with the big boss, trying to keep his mind on his job! He smiled weakly.

"Sit down, Tom, sit down! You look like you're about to shiver. You must be staying up too late at night." Marcus hit a button on his desk. "Hey, who's in this morning? Get me two cups of my special tea!" He released the button before whoever was in could answer and leaned back again. Tom sat down, facing him.

"Yeah, the boys like you," Marcus said, thoughtfully. "That's good, we all have to get along here. Are you used to the schedule around here yet?"

"Yes, I think so," Tom answered. "It's pretty simple to remember, and I don't mind the overtime."

"Good, good! And you get along with my boys? Johnny, Al, Frank?"

Tom nodded, saved from voicing an opinion when Alex came in with two mugs of steaming tea. He took one and sipped it. It tasted strange, not like any tea he ever had before. He realized that it must be one of those herbal mixtures that was sold through the case out front.

"You want anything else, Mr. Marcus?"

"No. And I don't want to be disturbed while I talk to Tom here, OK?"

"You got it, boss."

Tom smiled at the exchange. It must be great to have men like that at your beck and call, he reflected. To have a whole gym full of hunky men who called you "sir" and always "Mr. Marcus," and "boss," and got you drinks. He watched Alex leave, closing the door behind him.

"Yeah, so they tell me you're a good kid, Tom. You work hard, you put in your time, and you don't have to be told more then once how to do something." Marcus stood up, drinking his tea. "That tells me that you're going to train very well. because the key to doing these things right isn't having expensive equipment or the right genes, or the right clothes. It's personal dedication. It's doing what your trainer tells you, even if you don't understand why. It's having the discipline to do your workouts, no matter how you feel that day, or what you'd rather be doing." He stared at Tom directly. "Do you know what I mean?"

"I ... I think so, Mr. Marcus," Tom started to say. But the bodybuilder stopped him.

"No! That's the wrong attitude. You say, Yeah, Mr. Marcus, I know, or you say, No, Mr. Marcus, explain it to me again. Otherwise, you're copping out."

"Well ... yeah, I understand. My friend used to say the same things." Tom's heart twisted a little when he thought of Scott.

"Then he knew what it took. And I think you know what it takes, Tom. I think you know real well. You can't lie to me about it, I see the way you look at me, and the way you look at some of the boys here. You want to look like them, you want to build up. And you want real men to teach you, too, don't you?" Marcus leaned his hip back against the desk, directly in front of Tom. His voice was silky and deep, and the settling of his body made a clear outline of muscles and flesh against his clothes, and Tom's mouth went suddenly dry.

What is he saying, Tom asked himself furiously. Is he saying what I'm hearing? Oh, God, this is too fucking much for one morning! But everything about the way Marcus moved, and the new purr in his voice, screamed that he was willing to ... that he wanted Tom to ...

"You see," Marcus continued, "real men don't need fancy things to get them where they need to go. The best thing a builder needs is a good personal trainer. Someone he trusts absolutely. Someone who knows what's best for him. That's why champions come out of little places like this, and not those big, colorful candyland joints with all the pretty boys dancing around in their tights.

"This is the kind of place I started out in, and this is where I train world champions, kid. You want to see what I did with a good trainer and a lot of personal discipline?"

Tom nodded, not trusting his voice.

Marcus stood up straight and began to unbutton his shirt. His chest appeared from behind it, a tanned, massive block of flesh. As his hands went lower, he pulled the shirt out of his pants and shook it down over his broad shoulders.

Oh, God, but he was beautiful! Tom's head reeled as he drank in the sight of the torso that had won so many international awards. Big, and broad, and so masculine! Tom's hands let go of the cup, and he felt it leave them, heard it hit the floor, and heard Marcus' laugh as though it was all happening at a distance.

Marcus stepped away from the desk, and stood, his pose an arrogant invitation. Tom got up and walked over to him and stood in front of him, unsure as to what to do. Then, Marcus reached out and grabbed Tom by the hair and pulled him into his chest, drawing him to a nipple. Tom went joyfully.

CHAPTER FOUR

IV.

Tom stood, crushed by one of Marcus' arms, his mouth pressed into a chest that was firm with muscle. He took one nipple into his mouth and licked at it and sucked, and moaned. His earlier spasm of pleasure was forgotten, and lust rose in him like fevered blood.

Marcus laughed again, and dragged Tom's mouth over to the other nipple. "Good," he rumbled, "good!" And Tom's hips shook at the praise and he pressed himself even closer to the big man, tasting his clean flesh, loving it, pleasing it.

"Good boy," Marcus said, pulling Tom's head back for a moment. "Now show me how much you love this body. Really love it ..." He lifted one powerful arm and pressed Tom's face into the pit with one hand, like bringing a dog's nose to a bowl, and Tom dove in like the starved young animal he was! He thrust his tongue into the recess and washed it along the curves, tasting clean flesh not spoiled by chemicals or artificial scents. This was the smell of a man, the taste of his skin, his clear, honest smell. And when he was dragged to the other side, he went with a whimper of pleasure.

Marcus took as much as he liked, and then pulled Tom away from him. He laughed at the disappointed look on the boy's face, and let go of him. Tom tried to move closer, but Marcus held one hand up.

"You wait until I tell you to, boy," he said, carefully. "I'm in charge here, got it?"

"Yes ... yessir," Tom said, his mouth filled with the man's taste and his brain filled with his image.

"Good boy." Marcus grinned, and hooked his thumbs in his belt. "Then come here and get my shoes off. We're going to do this right."

Tom fumbled in his anxiety and heat, but he managed to kneel and take the polished black shoes off Marcus' feet, one at a time. The looming presence of the man standing above him was enough to make him break out in a sweat. The closeness of those powerful thighs and the tantalizing bulge between his legs combined to make the poor young man tremble with anticipation. He put the shoes over to one side and Marcus nodded when he made to take off the man's socks as well.

"Go ahead, Tom. If you're going to get this body, you're going to have to show that you love every inch of it. Get your mouth down there. I want to feel your lips. Kiss them, Tom. Show me how much you love me."

The hypnotic power of Marcus' voice brought Tom's head down over the bare feet, and he groveled like a dog and pressed his lips to them. Again, the sense of well-being flooded him; here too was the mark of a man, the smell and taste of one. Bent double, his dick pressed painfully against him, Tom licked and kissed Marcus' feet. Above him, he heard the clinking sound of a belt buckle being undone, and the sensuous sound of the leather slipping through the belt loops. He looked up to see the man drop the belt and beckon to him.

"You've got the right attitude, my boy," Marcus said, with satisfaction. "Get up here and get closer to what you really want."

Tom moved eagerly, and at the older man's direction, opened the trousers and lowered them over the strong hips and the thick, barrel shaped thighs.

Marcus wasn't wearing anything under the pants.

Tom stopped his sensual movements in absolute, amazed horror ... and hunger.

Ron Marcus hefted his machine up in one hand, and shook it temptingly in Tom's face. "I didn't tell you to stop, boy. Get them off. You'll get enough of this, when I let you."

Tom shuddered and continued to undress the man. Was his mouth actually watering? He had never seen a cock so huge, so beautiful! It was thick, and heavy looking, running with curving veins, the head a perfect plum shape. As Marcus lifted one foot and then the other, he grinned at the shaking youth on the floor before him, and turned slightly away. He stood, free and naked, his splendid body all the badges of honor a man could bear, and Tom's open-mouthed admiration was just a replay of every proper sexual encounter Marcus had ever had. Once again, the inferior was about to worship the superior. Once again, he was going to make an acolyte out of an unbeliever. But with an important twist.

"Come to me, Tommy boy. Come and taste this body."

"Oh, yeah," Tom moaned. He stumbled forward, and Marcus backed away, turning again, until Tom had to literally crawl after him. Tom couldn't think any more. Here was a million wet dreams come true, here was his man, his god, and all he could do was reach out and kiss those strong legs. Lick at those curved, oaken thighs. He hung onto the man like he was embracing a statue of inhuman beauty, and Marcus encouraged him with small words, crooning praise.

"That's it, Tom. Yes, that's it. Now come up here ... and worship." Marcus lifted his cock up to leave his heavy balls for Tom's attention, and Tom went for them like a boozer to drink. But at the last minute, Marcus caught Tom by the hair and held him firmly.

"Gently," he cautioned. "With reverence. I don't want you to suck my balls, little boy, I want you to show me that you love them. Start."

Tom waited until Marcus guided him to that dark, furry space between his legs, and hesitantly reached out with his tongue. The twin sacs that hung beneath the machine were worthy of worship, he thought, his first conscious thought in some time. They needed to be touched and licked, and kissed, the softness of his lips against the softness of their heavy curves. He mouthed them with full reverence, and when Marcus' hand urged him closer in, he breathed the rich, heavy scent of manhood and drank in the overwhelming feeling of being surrounded by masculine energy. He wrapped his arms around one of Marcus' thighs and gently took those hairy balls in his mouth, first one, and then the other. He let his mouth open wide to take them in, and washed his tongue over them with gentle, wide, wet strokes.

"Good," Marcus said again, enjoying the feel of the young man, and the sense of worship that came from him. "Now we'll see if you can do a real man's job. Get your mouth over here."

Tom left those fat balls with some regret. His own spit dribbled from his face involuntarily when the machine was lowered to his eye level.

Oh my God, I'll never be able to take that, he thought with a slight moan. It's too thick! And too long! And now, harder than it had been before, it was even more intimidating. He started to open his mouth to say something, but as soon as his lips parted, Marcus aimed and pushed the plum-shaped head of that monster cock against them. His hand took hold of Tom's head by a convenient handful of hair, and he drew Tom to him as he pushed.

"That's it, little boy, take my dick. You can't take it all, I know, not yet, but you're going to try, aren't you? Open wide, that's a good boy, and take it in, just the head for now ... that's it...."

Tom fought two opposing needs, the need to take this thing and be damned, and the sudden need to be free! But Marcus was relentless, and impossibly strong. When Tom's hands braced against those muscular thighs, it was like pressing against a stone wall. And Marcus held a firm grip on Tom's head, and would not let him move a single inch. And that cock! It filled his mouth, and pressed deeper, his tongue barely able to move around it. The feel was that of a silken battering ram, or the cock of some kind of god. In the end, Tom gave up trying to get away for the need to feel more of it in his mouth, the need to feel Marcus pushing it, sliding it deeper, until the head hit the back of his throat. He tried to draw breath through his nose, panting, and even though it was difficult, he also pushed himself forward.

"That's good, that's a nice try ... now let's see if you've got what it takes, cocksucker." Easily, Marcus shifted and thrust several inches of his machine into Tom's open mouth, slamming the head into the back of his throat.

Tom's mouth felt like it was stretched around a tree limb, his lips were pulled back, his tongue trapped on the underside of the monstrous invasion. The slam into the back of his throat brought unwilling tears to his eyes, and as he struggled, unable to breathe, he dimly heard Marcus chuckling. Yes, the powerful man was amused by Tom's feeble attempts to get away.

Carefully, Marcus pulled his shaft back, allowed Tom to take one gasping breath, and then slammed it back in. This time Tom groaned, and the vibration of the sound ran through Marcus' cock like a gentle tease. He sighed, and repeated the motion, getting the same result.

"You can't take all of it now," Marcus noted, not allowing Tom to draw away or take much of a breath. "But you'll learn. Soon, you'll be able to open up and take it down like any good whore. Because you want to, don't you? I can see it in your baby-blue eyes, my little cocksucker. Oh, yes, I like it when you gag like that. It fells really good on the head of my cock.... Let's do that again...." He began to fuck Tom's face, still not penetrating to the full length of the machine, but filling the youth anyway.

Tom stopped struggling because it cost him too much air. Instead, he allowed Marcus to control his head, and took a breath when he could, tears spilling down his face. The crooning encouragement of the large man seemed to be half endearment and half humiliation.

What is he doing, he cried to himself. I can't take it! Doesn't he realize? But I ... I want it! Oh God, he's incredible, he's so perfect! He's so huge! But it hurts, oh, God, I can't breathe, please, please finish, please ...

And then, suddenly, the cock was taken away. Tom gasped for air, and fell forward as Marcus took a step back. On his hands and knees, he leaned forward, trembling and shivering as Marcus watched him. Then, intimidated by the silence and confused by the sudden withdrawal, Tom looked wearily up to see his god before him.

Marcus was standing, legs spread and planted firmly, with one hand stroking the machine that had just mercilessly battered Tom's throat. His entire body shone with a slight sheen of sexual excitement, his grin and his piercing eyes mocking Tom and inviting him at the same time.

"You want my cum, Tom?" Marcus asked, his hand continuing to work. "You want my hot jism?"

"Yes," Tom croaked out, aware that his throat was sore from the face fucking and his voice broken by his own desire. "Yes, God, yes...."

"But how can you do that, my little cocksucker? You can't take it all the way down your tight throat ... yet. And I know you can't take me up your asshole ... yet. So tell me why I should bother giving you my cum, when you're such a fucking useless piece of shit." Marcus' voice was hard, but Tom didn't hear the harshness. Instead, he moaned, mentally agreeing with the man.

He'll never let me do this again, he thought, lowering his head. I can't do it! He's so fucking hot, and I can't even take him, how the hell can I even hope? The thought of the searing pain of being fucked by this man sent a rush of pleasure and horror through the young man. The image of being pinned down by his bulk and strength, being wrapped in that muscular embrace and really fucked, fucked until he screamed, hit Tom like a slap across his face. He raised his head and whispered, "Please!", not knowing whether he was begging for the pain, or for a solution. Marcus smiled and beckoned.

"Crawl to me, little pig. Get your face under me."

Tom did, the shame of it bringing fire to his cheeks. But when he reached the man, and stopped and turned his face up, his mouth actually watered. Between his legs, his dick felt like iron. He knew that he had already spent a quantity of precum, and the cool wetness was an agonizing irritant.

Marcus rubbed his cock against Tom's up-turned face, first gently, and then with force. Still smiling, he used it like a fleshy club and slapped Tom with it, against his cheeks and his lips, until Tom tasted blood in his mouth. Tom tried to open his mouth to capture it again, but Marcus with-held, teasing the boy, and then punishing him for reaching. Each slap was an empty thud against Tom's brain, all he thought of was the silken feel-ing of that warm manflesh, the powerful thrusts that carried it to his throat, and when he saw that Marcus was pumping away at it with more intensity, suddenly Tom knew what he was going to do.

"Close your eyes and mouth," Marcus growled. "Since you're not good enough to take me all the way, I don't see why I should bother fucking you. But I've got plenty of juice, boy. I can waste some on you today."

Tom moaned again and did as he was told, and the world shrank to the sound of Marcus' hand sliding back and forth, and the smell of his body, and the feel of the floor beneath Tom's knees.

"Tell me you want it, boy. Ask me for it. Beg me."

"Please!" The word leapt out without any thought behind it. "Please, please give me your cum!" Right now, Tom felt like there wasn't any-thing in the world he wanted more. What if Marcus took it away? He panicked. "I want it so bad ... I need to feel it, please, I'll do anything, suck your cock, lick your balls, your ass, please ..."

The first splatter of hot wetness hit Tom on his forehead, and he cut off his pleas with a sigh of gratification. But it didn't stop there. Forceful splashes hit his eyelids and his nose and cheeks, and began to dribble down his face to his neck. And it kept coming! The smell of it was thick and overwhelming, and as Marcus decorated Tom's face with gobs of it, Tom gloried in the bath. Trickles of cum began to run underneath his shirt collar.

Finally, Marcus was finished. He stepped away from Tom again, leaving the young man on his knees, his face and throat covered with trails of his potent manjuice.

It took Tom a while to begin to recover. To his dismay and embarrassment, he found that he had cum sometime, but he didn't remember it! The pool of wetness between his thighs was proof, though. He opened his eyes finally, just in time to see the damp towel that Marcus tossed him, and weakly, he used it to wipe his face. He felt dazed, and his knees were stiff all of a sudden. And he was suddenly very ashamed at the way he had behaved.

Marcus was sitting again, dressed in a light robe. "You have potential, Tom," he said amiably. "But you've got to learn how to take me all the way. Next time, I'll really fuck your face. You'll get used to it. I think I'll save your ass for a little while, give you some time to get it open for me if you want. You should thank me; usually I don't give my boys that option."

"What?" Tom asked, standing up. He had wiped away most of the cum, but cooling lines of it trailed his chest and back. He shivered. "Uh ... I don't ..."

"Sit down, Tom, and I'll explain things to you.

That's it, sit down, you'll feel better in a minute. Let me make things easy for you. You belong to me, now. You know it's right. You want it, and I'm willing to train you. But the cost of my training, in this and other things, is your absolute obedience. In all things. Understand?"

"No!" Tom said. "I mean, yeah, I understand, but I don't agree. I took the job, and yeah, I'd like to, um, well, you know...."

"Get fucked regularly," Marcus filled in with a cruel smile. "Yes, you need it badly. But I don't give that away for nothing. If you obey me and follow my directions, not only will you get the time here at the gym and the body that you dream of, but you'll also get regular tastes of my cock, and get your ass filled the way you need it."

Tom blushed. Scott had never been so brutally direct with him. And the need was strong in him right now. But not that strong.

"Sorry. I didn't come to work here to be a ... a hustler. I guess I'll have to look for a new job. I'm sorry, Mr. Marcus...."

Marcus laughed softly and leaned back. "Not as sorry as you're going to be, young Tommy. I didn't offer you a choice here. I told you what's going to happen."

"Yeah, well, I'm sorry, but it's not," Tom retorted, standing up. "Now if you're not going to pay me, I'll just go clear out my locker and ..."

"You'll sit down and you'll *never* raise your voice to me again, you filthy little cheap cocksucker," Marcus declared. His eyes sharpened in anger, and he hit the desk with the flat of his hand. "Get your ass in that chair! I am not finished with you!"

"No! I'm outa here!" Tom took the two steps to the door and tried the handle, but it seemed to be locked. He tugged harder on it, and cursed.

"Alex locked it on his way out," Marcus offered. "You're getting me angry, Tom. Get your ass in that chair right now."

Tom turned around, and put his back to the door. "You better let me out, Mr. Marcus. I swear, I'll call the cops." He felt fear rising up in him when Marcus stood up, but the man only picked up his clothing and began to dress again.

"Yes, you might do that. But if you did, you should make them some popcorn." He pulled on his pants and the machine went back into hiding.

"Wha ..?" Tom asked.

"Popcorn. It's the usual snack food served when watching movies, isn't it?" Marcus put his shirt back on and began to fasten the buttons. "If you call the police and tell them some fantastic story about how the award-winning humanitarian Ron Marcus wouldn't let you out of his office, I'd just have to run a little private movie I made, and show them what a greedy little punk you really are."

He turned back to the desk and picked up a remote control unit, which he clicked at the pile of stereo and television equipment in one corner. Tom shook and his mouth went dry.

"You ... you didn't ..."

"Yes, I did. Made a tape of the whole thing. And one look at it will make any New York cop laugh until his belt falls off, kiddo. He'll be likely to take *you* in, if you bother him enough." Marcus bent down and picked up his belt. A small whirring sound suddenly stopped, and he used the remote to turn on the video screen and start scanning through the tape.

Tom felt like throwing up. There, quite clearly, was him, dopey with lust and worship, groveling, begging, licking and sucking, kissing the man's feet, for crying out loud! The scenes flashed by, colorful images of male lust interspersed with lines of static, everything in fast-forward. It was almost comic, but it was real. Tom Kake, all-American boy, worshipping the body of another man, sucking his balls and cock. Without the slightest hint of force of compulsion.

Because there wasn't any, he bitterly reminded himself. His stomach twisted into knots.

"Now, I ordered you to sit down, Tom, and you still haven't," Marcus said calmly. "I'm going to have to punish you for that." He continued to scan through the tape, slowing it down from time to time, and then finally getting to the part where he came all over Tom's screwed up face. Tom watched, helpless with horror, fascinated by the sight of him being drenched with the juices he could still smell and feel on his body.

Marcus turned to face him when the tape was over. "So that I won't have to explain all of this more then once and let you try to disobey me again, I'll give you the whole story now. As long as you remain a good boy, come to work and do your job, you continue to get paid. As long as you do everything I say, whether it's cleaning out my toilet or taking my dick down your throat, you get private training, after-hours access to the gym, and the secrets of becoming a real man. And as long as you shut up about the deal and keep your word, I keep this tape under lock and key. The minute you try to run, or try to tell anyone with the intent to hurt me or cause me embarrassment, this tape goes out. It goes to mom and dad in that shitcaked town you come from, to grandma and grandpa, it goes to any other member of your family I can find, it goes to your old preacher, your Sunday school teacher, and it goes to whatever amateur fuck video place I can peddle it to."

He put the remote away and doubled the belt in his hands. "Do you understand?"

Tom shook his head, tears forming again. How could this be happening? What was going on? "No! Please don't…. I won't go to the cops, I won't tell anyone, just let me go, I swear I won't say anything!"

"Too late, Tom. Because now I want you. I want to make a proper man out of you, Tom, and one day you will thank me for it. But right now, I'm going to teach you never to disobey me on a direct order."

Tom tried to squirm away, but for all of his bulk, Marcus was a fast man. He reached out and grabbed Tom by the collar of his T-shirt and shook him.

"If you make me tie you up for this, I'm going to make sure you regret it for the rest of your life, do you understand?" he demanded, dragging Tom back over to the chair. "Answer me, idiot!"

"Yes! Yes!" Tom tried to shield his head, but Marcus wasn't interested in it. Instead, the body-builder bent Tom forward over the back of the chair.

"Take your pants down, boy. Get 'em down around your knees, and then grab the arms of the chair." Marcus ran the leather belt through his hands, waiting, while Tom did as he was told. Tom was wearing clean but worn jockey shorts under his jeans, and with a soft curse, Marcus took hold of the cotton fabric and tore them off, making Tom cry out. Wadded in his hand, Marcus felt their dampness, and walked around to face Tom.

"Well, you little cocksucking fairy, you came in your shorts, didn't you? When was it, when you were choking on my meat, or when you realized how much you belonged to me?" He tossed them in Tom's face and walked back behind him.

"What are you gonna do," Tom asked, nervously. "Please ... please don't fuck me, it's been a while, I can't take it...."

"I'll fuck you whenever the fuck I want to, cocksucker."

But he didn't fuck him. Instead, Marcus used the belt and relentlessly beat him. Tom tried to take it as well as the man he had seen with Frank earlier that morning, but it was impossible. Each sharp blow to his ass seemed to go through his entire body, and he was crying out and twisting away from them in no time. It was a short beating, no more then fifteen or sixteen strokes, but each one seemed to leave a line of fire across his ass, and made it all the more difficult to hold his position. But he was afraid. Afraid of what Marcus might do if he moved.

"You know what this is for, Tommy? Because you didn't listen to me. When I tell you to do something, from now on, you do it." Marcus punctuated his lecture with blows from the belt until Tom apologized and promised to be more obedient in the future.

Finally, when it was over, he felt a weird kind of gratitude flood him, and he was ashamed all over again. He heard Marcus order him to get his jeans back on, and not to wear jockey shorts any more. He did as he was told, and mutely accepted the envelope that Marcus passed him.

"There's your pay, Tommy. Be good and do the right thing. I know you will. You do really want this, boy, I can tell. You came to me of your own free will, and you will thank me one day. But now, you better get back to work. I'll see you bright and early Monday morning."

That day was inhumanly long. Mentally numb and physically sore, Tom went about his chores with a blank look on his face, and had to be reminded about what he was doing several times. He avoided the pool room and showers as long as he could, and by the end of the day, when he was cleaning up, he broke down and cried, alone in the tiled private showers where Frank Dobbs had beaten and fucked another man that morning. It was hard to believe that this was how his day had started. Tom cried like he did when he realized how alone he was after Scott left. He cried for the injustice done to him and for the fact that he couldn't see a way out.

After a while, though, he washed his face and did his job and left at the usual time, doing his best to appear nonchalant. *That was really weak*, he said to himself as he walked out into the night air. *I can't afford to do that again. I have to figure out how to get out of this.*

He walked through the streets, his hands in his pockets, the envelope of cash burning against his leg. It's my pay, he reminded himself. I earned it with hard work. I need it, to pay the rent and get clothes and food. It has nothing to do with ... what Marcus did.

Perhaps the worst thing about thinking about what to do was the shameful way he continued to think of Mr. Marcus. Despite the cruelty, despite the blackmail, something primal inside of him hungered for the kind of man Marcus was. A masculine, muscular, powerful and confident topman. A man who took what he wanted. A man with a cock that would choke ...

Tom blushed suddenly and tried to turn his mind back to the problems at hand.

He couldn't just walk away, not while Marcus had a copy of that tape. Maybe one day he would come out to his family ... well, at least to Mom ... but not that way. And of course, Marcus had his home address, it would be so easy to track down other members of his family back home. Why that tape would just about kill grandpa Kake, with all his talk about "city faggots" and "homo boys"! And what if one of his cousins got hold of it and showed it to some kids?

I'd never be able to go home, Tom admitted to himself. *Oh, why didn't I take that job flipping hamburgers! Now I'm in shit up to my ears*. He continued his walk, trying to think, and ate his first good meal since Rodriguez had bought him lunch, and then went home. And even though the night was early, he went to bed right away.

And slept like a baby.

CHAPTER FIVE

CHAPTER FIVE

V.

On Saturday morning, Tom found himself standing on the edge of his bathtub to see if he could get a glimpse of his rear end in the mirror over his sink. There were a few red lines painted over the curves of his ass, but no heavy bruises. Remembering the scene in the private shower room, he realized that his own beating must have been comparatively light. He didn't know how to feel about that except relieved.

I'm such a coward, he thought as he pulled his clothing on. But what could I have done? Marcus would have creamed me! Shit, all he has to do is look at me funny and I turn into jello.

The lump of cash in his pocket felt hard against his leg, and he pulled it out to count it.

Even with the cash advance taken out, there was enough there to do some real grocery shopping and get a new pair of sneakers. Rent wasn't due for another three weeks. He did a little mental figuring and split the cash in half, and shoved one pile under his mattress, pushing it toward the center of the bed.

I can think while I'm out shopping, he thought, putting his jacket on.

It was a beautiful day. The air was crisp, and the streets were filled with kids out of school. He walked two blocks out of his way to avoid passing the gym, knowing that it was open and dreading the thought of someone seeing him and stopping to talk. Instead, he headed west and was soon swallowed into the life and activity of the Village.

For over two hours he window-shopped, looking at various stores, peering through glass to examine all kinds of merchandise. He wandered through a huge music store, and wondered how long it would take him to save for a stereo, and stared at the prices on "designer footwear" in horror. Again, he reflected on how expensive living in the city could be, and the thought sobered him. Everything always brought him back to his current predicament, and nothing seemed to ease it.

And Rodriguez tried to warn me, he remembered, passing by the restaurant where the Latino had bought him lunch. Why didn't I listen? The image of Will floated into his mind, pumped up and sweaty, that ink-black hair curling against his body, and Tom felt a jolt of sharp longing. Then he looked back at the restaurant, and turned back.

100

It took him a few minutes to find the waiter
who had served them. It took a few more minutes
to get the information that if Will was going to be
in today, he would be in sometime around 4 PM.
Tom thanked the man and on an impulse, gave
him a five-dollar bill. Instantly, the man was all
smiles, and Tom was ushered out with a strong
invitation to come again, soon.

Money solves everything, Tom thought. Well,
almost everything. It won't get me out of this. But
maybe Will has a way out.

He passed some time in a bookstore, and then
wandered aimlessly, never very far from the
restaurant. It was a beautiful day, very sunny
and slightly warm for the season, and the streets
were crowded. He examined piles of magazines
and books laid out on blankets and card tables on
the sidewalk, and listened to the street vendors
haggle with their potential customers. If his life
weren't so messed up, it would have been a near
perfect day!

At a little before four in the afternoon, he took
up a post opposite the restaurant, and resolved to
wait until dark. It wasn't necessary. Will got out
of a taxi at precisely 4:12, and turned toward the
restaurant at once.

I guess when you've got to keep up a clientele,
you make sure you're a regular somewhere, Tom
reflected. Or maybe this is just one place he goes
a lot. Maybe he has lots of places where the people know him. Maybe the gym is one! Tom crossed
the street, avoiding the traffic with ease, and followed Will into the place, not hailing him. Inside,
Will was already heading for a table, and Tom followed him and slid into a chair opposite him. Will

looked up, not so much surprised that he was joined, but surprised that it was Tom.

"Hi," Tom said, suddenly aware that his usual grin didn't look natural. He tried it anyway, and then coughed to hide his discomfort. "Mind if I join you?"

Will shrugged, and beckoned to the waiter. A coffee landed in front of him almost instantly, and he poured cream into it. "You're here, I won't throw you out," he said, his voice chilly. "What's up?"

Tom was taken aback by the near-hostility in Will's voice, but he buried his eyes in the menu and controlled himself. "Um, nothing much. I ... I just wanted to see you, I guess. Talk a little, maybe."

"So talk."

Tom's heart sank. But he kept his cool and scanned the menu, not really reading anything. So much for any help from him, he thought. But what was I thinking anyway? He tried to warn me, and I ignored him. Now, he thinks I'm an asshole.

Which I am! New in town, I can't even figure out who's real and who's fake, and who wants what from me, and who's lying....

"You gonna eat, or read?" Tom looked up to find the waiter standing there, pen poised, and realized that Will had already ordered while he was lost in self pity. He looked back down at the menu, and then back up at the waiter, and then Will sighed.

"Make the same for him," he said, pulling the menu out of Tom's hands. "And a coke."

"Thanks, I think. What did you order?"

"What do you care? Did you really just happen to hit this place same time I did so you could sample the excellent cuisine?" Will's voice rose in a sneer. He drank his coffee, staring at Tom until the young man dropped his eyes. "You wanted to talk, well here I am, talk. Or just tell me what's up. What did you do today?" He leaned back.

Tom almost sprang up to leave, but he stayed where he was and looked back at Will. He even managed to take a sip from his coke. "I went shopping. I was going to by new sneakers, but they're too expensive."

Will's dark eyes lit up in light astonishment, and then he half smiled. "OK, we can talk about shopping, man. Your problem is that you're in the wrong neighborhood. Too many yuppies up here. You gotta head downtown more, or way uptown, go to one of those big discount places, or check out some guy in a van with some hot shoes, and get a nice pair for maybe twenty dollars."

"Really? Can you tell me where? And how to get there?"

"Oh yeah, sure. Getting quality stuff real cheap is one of my specialties." Will suddenly grinned, and Tom felt a little better. Even if he couldn't help me, he thought, looking into his eyes, he's probably nice to know. I want him to like me.

"Where are you living?" Will asked, just as the food arrived. "What neighborhood?"

Tom told him, told him about his desire to live in "The Village," and the ad that said something that was exactly what he wanted but not exactly what he got. He even told him about the green hospital sheets, which made him laugh.

"Welcome to New York, man," the darker man

said. "You got hooked like a fish. But hey, lots of folks want to live in that area, you know? It's very funky. Lotsa good clubs down there, new music. You just got to get used to heading in some other direction when you're out shopping. Otherwise, you'll go broke real fast."

"I noticed. That's why I needed a job so fast—" It slipped out without his thinking about it, and Tom found himself stammering and blushing. "I mean ... I was really broke...."

Rodriguez nodded. "Yeah, and you took the job, like I told you you shouldn't. So you got money now, right? Everything's just fine now, right?"

Tom dropped his eyes again and toyed with his food. This time the impulse to run was stronger, but the energy just wasn't there.

"Happy with the job? Like the boss?" Will's voice was just like the belt that Marcus used on him, sharp and stunning in its intensity. Tom's head drooped lower.

"I wish I'd listened to you," he said softly.

"Yeah well, it's too fucking late, isn't it?"

To his horror, Tom felt a tear escape. He tried to hold it back, and failing that, he blinked hard and rubbed it quickly, like he was taking care of a sudden itch.

"You poor sucker, what the fuck's the matter with you? Don't go all to pieces, man. That is *not* the correct attitude. You think you're the only idiot Marcus has ever done this too? Come on, let's go. I'll tell you a story or two, and you'll see just what kind of deep shit you're in. Because you are in it, boy, up to your fucking eyeballs. Lucky for you, I like blonds. Hey, Rudi! Check, man."

Will paid the bill and hailed a cab outside the

restaurant. During the ride downtown, he pointed out the places he had mentioned, places to buy clothing and shoes and housewares and stereos. Tom went mutely, half-stunned by Will's sudden change from hostility to friendliness, overwhelmed by the sudden generosity and embarrassed over his near breakdown. But Will never mentioned it along the way.

They went into a neighborhood that sounded a lot like Tom's, but looked different. There were more signs in different languages, and more dark corners and alleyways. Radios blared from windows and passing cars. Vacant lots dotted the landscape.

They got out in front of what looked like an industrial building, and Rodriguez led Tom into a mildewed hallway and up shoddy, noisy stairs. On the third landing was a huge steel door, and it took several keys to get it to open. But the inside was an amazing contrast to the outside.

It was the first time Tom had seen a real New York loft space. A nice one. Polished wood floors invited them into a sweepingly long room, leading to large windows at the front. Low walls, hardly even room dividers, were painted deep, warm colors, and hung with striped blankets and pictures in silver frames. A small kitchen was off to the left when they walked in.

"This is my place," Will said, closing the door behind them. "I had a friend come in and decorate for me. He's real good. He usually charges thousands of dollars to do this shit, you know? But he liked me." He smiled, white teeth flashing. "To tell you the truth, I was so happy to leave home, I would have lived in this place before they put the

105

floors in and fixed it up. Man, it was a sorry sight, let me tell you. And it had rats, mice, you name it. Now, I got a pair of cats, and they take care of the place." He looked around. "They're shy, they'll come out later. You want a beer or something?"

"Yeah, I'd love one," Tom said eagerly. "This place is great! I could never afford something like this...."

"Oh, they're not bad," Will said, ducking into the kitchen area. "But look at the neighborhood I'm in, man. Not exactly a family place, you know? And we get the cops in here, once, twice a week, just to clean out the junkies from the lobby downstairs. Man, I thought I left all that shit at home."

He popped the cap off two bottles of cold beer and pointed into the loft. "Sit down, man. It's story time."

"Where's home?" Tom asked, taking a seat in a large, comfortable chair. The beer felt chilly in his hand, smooth down his throat.

"The Bronx. Family still lives there, mostly. I've been out of the house for ..." he did some mental figuring, "almost seven years now. Since I was fifteen."

"Wow," Tom said, genuinely impressed. "You've been here since you were a kid?"

"No, stupid, not here. This is new, maybe eight, nine months old. Before that, I lived in a place a couple of blocks from here, it was terrible. Roaches everywhere, man. The other people in the building were filthy!" He spat the word out, and Tom realized that Will Rodriguez was a very fastidious man. He smiled slightly, and drank some more beer.

"And then before that, I lived uptown, in Chelsea,

106

with these other guys. That was about two years ago. Before that ... I lived wherever. In the street, in shelters, in abandoned cars, under bridges, with overnight tricks ... wherever. Sometimes with friends. For a while, I even lived at the gym. I mean, I slept there. Marcus let me, sometimes, when it was cold. That was how I met him."

Tom sat up, leaning forward. Will put his beer bottle down to pet a single Siamese cat that had quietly entered the area, and he gathered his thoughts.

"Marcus worked you over, right?"

Tom nodded.

"Did he fuck you?"

Tom started to shake his head, but stopped in mid-motion. "Uh, well, not like ..."

"Did he fuck you *anywhere*, Blondie? Mouth, ass, armpit, whatever." Will said, in exasperation.

Tom nodded.

"Well, welcome to the fucking club, man. You're probably the twentieth, maybe the fiftieth young guy he's done it to. No one knows for sure, you know? But every working stiff at the gym, every goddamn one, even that fucking ugly asshole Frank, has taken that horsecock at least a dozen times. Probably much more. And he gets new meat every week or so, customers, clients, hustlers, street trash, you name it. *Caracho!*" He made a spitting noise and the cat jumped away.

"He filmed me," Tom said.

"Yeah, he does that. And he told you he was gonna mail it home to mama if you told, right? Or if you left?"

"Yeah. It's a pretty good trick, I guess," he noted. "I fell for it."

107

"Hey, everyone falls for it, man. And don't think he won't do it, either. Just last week, he sent one of his homemade movies out to the entire fucking family of this Chinese kid that had your job before you. And lately, he sends it to some porno guy too, and who knows where the fuck it'll end up, right?" Will was genuinely mad, and Tom could hear the same frustration in his voice as he heard in his own.

"So you can't suggest some way for me to get out of this, huh?" he asked, leaning back again.

"Ha! No way, man, unless you wanna find out where he keeps those tapes and steal back your own. And believe me, men have tried. This straight guy, real beauty, man, he tried that. Tried to break in a couple of times, and the alarm systems always held. Then he comes in one day with a gun, tries to get Marcus to open the safe. Meanwhile, Frank comes in with a fucking baseball bat, and it's all over. They worked that shit-head over until his own mama couldn't recognize him, man." Will shook his head, remembering. "It was pretty gruesome, let me tell you. They made a bunch of us look at him before they took him away. They didn't even call an ambulance or something, just took him away. And he never pressed charges or nothing."

Tom shivered. "Was he ... is he alive?"

"Yeah, I think so. Wasting is just not Marcus' style, you know? But he was messed up good."

"Who could fight against Mr. Marcus? No one would have a chance."

"Marcus isn't the fighter, my friend. It's Frankie boy who's the real motherfucker. How'd you think he got that pretty face? He used to be a boxer, and he was one of those special soldiers, you know? Green Beret, or some kind of shit like that. He's probably out of the army because he's a fucking psycho." He gestured strongly, and tossed back some beer. He was warming to his story.

"Yeah, he's the real killer when it comes to kicking ass. But he's Marcus' guy, all the way. And he's not too bright sometimes. So you got the psycho and the brains controlling him, man. It's a deadly combination."

"I can see that."

"But it's not the whole story. The managers, they're in on this, too."

"Alex and John?"

"Shit yeah. They started out like you, man. Marcus probably has movies all about them, too. But now they're not his fuckholes as much as they used to be. He likes his boys young and fresh, like you, Blondie."

Tom shivered again.

"You ain't alone. I was where you are, man. Only I was younger. And stupider." Will sat back and shifted in his seat, and then leapt up. "I'm gonna get the rest of the fucking six-pack, Blondie. You wanna join me in getting shitfaced?"

"Yeah!"

He returned with the beer and placed it between them. Instantly, another cat came out and rubbed herself on the cans, and then plopped herself down next to Tom's chair. Will opened another beer and collected his thoughts.

"I started hustling a long time ago," he said suddenly. "I dealt a little on the side, but it was just too dangerous. Besides, I didn't think of myself as a criminal, you know? I saw too many neighborhood boys die real young and get messed up real young. My own papa, he was a needle freak, probably dead now. I knew I liked boys when I was really little, played with some of the kids in my gang, until we knew what we were doing and stopped. In my neighborhood, the worst thing they can call you is *maricon*, you know, faggot. So I started running away, coming into the city. I'd meet older boys and men, they always gather together, you know? And they'd teach me things and pay me, and buy me things. If I showed up with new shoes or a new jacket, no one really noticed, or if they did, they thought I was dealing, or running, or watching for some dealer."

He paused to take another drink. "This went on for years, man. And I couldn't take being at home anymore. I have three sisters, and a brother, and my mama. I'm the oldest. Mama would always want me to watch the little ones, and I would always want to be off on my own. And she didn't like the idea that I was messing with drugs, and she used to yell all the time, man. So I spent more and more time away, and then I finally stopped going home. I mean, I still go see her." He looked up, making sure that Tom understood. "She's my mama, I love her, and I love my sisters and my little brother, but I would have gone crazy in that house. It was better to sleep on the street, man."

"That must have been tough."

Will shrugged. "It wasn't that bad. I had places to go. I even had my favorite social workers, they'd bring me sandwiches and condoms, and little booklets about their programs. And I had some regular customers, too; they'd take me home

110

when they could. One was a school teacher, his wife'd go away, and he'd bring me home. He was kinda stuffy, but he taught me how to eat in fancy restaurants, and how to dress really nice. He was kinky, too. Liked to dress me up in his wife's panties, and then I'd have to put them in his mouth before I fucked him." Will grinned at the memory. "That was some weird shit."

Tom laughed.

"And he wasn't the weirdest! So I have no regrets, you know? But then, it started to get dangerous. The trade was going down for a long time. And to tell you the truth, the better customers kept disappearing ... it was a real drag, man. One day they'd be there, and then they'd just stop coming around, and you'd hear ..." He paused again, started again. "And people were starting to get nasty, yelling at us from cars, throwing bottles and shit.... One guy I knew, a drag queen, they got him down on the piers, man, kicked the living shit out of him. I'd be afraid to get into someone's car. And then, even if I thought the guy was OK, suddenly, they'd wanna boogie without the scumbag, man, and I just don't do that. If I wanted a short life, I'd be dealing crack, OK? Plus, I realized that I was a topman, you know, and more guys are looking to fuck then get fucked. So times got tough. That's when I met Marcus."

He took a deep drink, and accepted the cat that leapt into his lap. "He picked me up on a really slow night. It was cold out, too, and I was trying to figure out where I was going to stay. By that time, I was ready to cut my fees if I could sleep over, you know? So this guy pulls up, and man, I know he's no bottom, but he asks if I'm looking for company, and I figure, he's gotta be rich, he knows the language, and he wants you for the night. You can take it one more time, if it means you're gonna be warm. I tell him that normally, I'm top, but he's so hot, you know, that it's OK.... Hey, he was a customer, OK?"

Tom's eyes widened. "It doesn't matter," he said softly. "He is hot."

"Well ... yeah. But you have to realize that I got a different perspective on him."

"Go on. Please."

"I was going to. What happened was that he took me home, and he showed me a good time. I mean, it was OK. He wasn't fucking brutal, you know? Later, I found out that he filmed it. When he says good-bye in the morning, he tells me where the gym is, and tells me I should come by and he'd give me some kind of really hot-shit training program, and maybe we could work it out in trade."

Will stood up and posed. "I wasn't always like this," he said proudly. "Couple of years ago, I was nothing, this greasy little spic kid, skinny body, soft shoulders. When he told me what he could do with my body, man, I was in heaven. I didn't walk, I fucking ran to the gym, that same day." He sat down, his face becoming more composed again. "I wanted it all. I wanted to look like a real man, a macho man, take my shirt off and make every women hot, every man jealous. So I ran. I ran straight to him."

"Hey, so did I...."

"Yeah, but you're a bottom, Blondie. Am I fucking right? You see a guy, when you want him, you want him to fuck you, right?"

Tom blushed.

"Well, I'm not, man. And I thought I'd maybe get used to it, or maybe he'd get tired, or maybe ... I don't know what I thought. I knew that once I looked right, I could set my own prices and top all the time, man. Guys pay good money for a topman that looks like this. My personal ads read some shit like, "muscular Latin lover," and they just come running!"

"Yeah," offered Tom, gulping down more beer.

"Well, I was looking at the future, but not where I was going. Marcus didn't get tired of me, he only got rougher. And kinkier. And more ... demanding. And then, he ... he'd bring Frank in to watch. And when I protested, he'd smack me around. And when I tried to leave, he showed me the tapes he made ... and you know what he said."

"Yeah."

"And I wasn't the first asshole to fall for it, and I'm sure as hell not the fucking last. And I gotta watch while he keeps on keepin' on, you know?"

They sat in silence for a few moments. The only sounds in the room were the muffled noises of the street and the loud purring of one of the cats. Tom looked at the intensely handsome man in front of him and sighed, struck both by the tragic tale he had just been told and the classic beauty of the storyteller. It would appear that Will couldn't come up with some easy solution for the problem if he was caught in it, too, but somehow, that made it easier for Tom to take. I wasn't the first, he thought, putting the empty bottle of beer down. Even Will fell for it....

"Hey," he said suddenly. "If you knew what he

113

was going to do, why didn't you just come out and say it? I would have believed you!"

"Would you have, man?" Will looked up, a sarcastic twist to his mouth. "The last time I tried that, the sucker went straight back to Marcus and asked him what the problem was between him and me. Just like that, man. 'Will Rodriguez is spreading nasty rumors about you, Mr. Marcus! Why would he do something like that?'" His voice scaled up in imitation of a real queen, and he waggled one wrist. Then, he dropped his voice back to normal. "The bastard thought he'd be doing me a favor, man. You wanna guess what happened? You wanna take a wild fucking guess how Marcus took this information?"

"Oh." Tom shrugged. "Well, I would have believed you."

"If you remember, Blondie, I fucking tried, OK? And you didn't. So you're Marcus' new boy, and that's that. But don't worry, he'll get tired of you when someone cuter comes long. And, if you do what he tells you, eat the right foods, do the right workout, take his fucking vitamins, hey, maybe you'll fill out and start looking like a hot dude yourself. Not a bad deal, huh?"

Will finished his beer and put the bottle down, brushing the cat off his lap. "But for now, maybe you got something else in mind? Like sucking my cock?"

Tom swallowed hard. "Wh-what?"

"Man, I could tell you were hot for me the first time we met. Now that you got my whole fucking life story, why don't you get your ass over here and do what you really want to do, huh?" Will put one hand over the bulge in his jeans and

114

squeezed. A curve of muscle showed through the artfully faded denim. "No charge man, not for you. I like little blond guys, myself. Like to see them sucking on my fat cock. So stop wasting my time, and either get over here, or get your ass home."

Tom went over to him. It was an easy choice. Dropping to his knees in front of the Latino's chair, he reached for the buttons of his fly and carefully opened them, while Will opened the last bottle of beer. "Yeah, that's it, Blondie. Nice and gentle, nice and polite. Get it out, man, and get it in." He took a long drink as Tom breathed in the heady scent of a hot man and reached into the folds of the jeans to wrap his fingers around a warm, pulsating tube of flesh.

Bringing it out was a task that actually made Tom's mouth water. It was not yet fully hard, but it was nice and juicy looking, and wonder of wonders, it was uncut! The fold of skin was not yet pulled back over the head, but edged it with an inviting ridge of soft flesh. Tom lowered his head into Will's lap and kissed his cock with a real reverence.

"Yeah, that's nice Blondie, real nice ... lemme feel your tongue, kiddo, lick me up and down, just like a lollipop, yeah, that's it, all the way, up and down...."

Tom followed the instructions eagerly, getting the taste of the man in his mouth, on his lips and tongue. He felt the fingers of Will's left hand stroking the side of his head and down by his ear, and he shivered with pleasure. Then, that hand went away, only to reappear on the cock he was busy licking. Will grasped it and lifted it up,

115

exposing a dark recess, still lost in the jeans, where tangled black hairs held a pair of sweaty balls.

"Get in there, Blondie. I want to feel you licking my *cojones* clean.... Get your tongue in there deep, man. Come and get it, man."

Tom dove in, his nose and mouth wedged under the fleshy base of Will's cock, his tongue darting into the tight space to lap at the twin spheres nestled there. Will slowly jacked his dick, running his hand over the silken areas washed by Tom's tongue, and he leaned back, pushing his hips forward to give Tom more space.

"Hey, you're not bad, Blondie," he sighed, tipping a little beer into his mouth. "What you don't have in talent, you make up for in ... enthusiasm, man. Yeah, that's right, keep showing that enthusiasm!" He laughed, and Tom felt the vibrations of the laugh through his stomach. But Tom didn't care. He was buried in his favorite place on a man, with the specter of a nice, uncut dick just over his face, and the promise of it in his mouth.

His oral attentions to Will's balls continued for some time, and Tom realized that Will had to be one of those men who like having their balls being paid attention to. That was nice, now that was fucking great!

Finally, Will pulled his head back and lowered his cock toward Tom's mouth. "That was real good, Blondie. Come on and take what you want now, wrap me up and take me down, man."

Tom opened his mouth, his lips smeared with his own spit and the sweat off Will's nuts, and sucked in the tan cock he was offered. His tongue instantly found that mysterious covering of flesh so lacking from most American men, and dived under it. Yes! That was it, finally, he had one, it was in his mouth, all his! The salty taste rushed into him like a hit from a popper, and he moaned around the cockhead.

"Hey, you're a real cheesehound, Blondie!" Will laughed again, and moved his hips forward. "Like your meat uncut, huh? Well, dive in, sucker, get a good taste, 'cause as soon as you do, I'm gonna find out what the rest of your cocksucking mouth is like. Come on, lick it up, get your fucking mouth in there, and watch your fucking teeth, man. If I feel your fucking teeth on my hood, no more cock for you tonight...."

Tom certainly didn't want that! He concentrated on using his lips and tongue and kept his teeth sheathed, and did as he was told. He didn't just lick and suck at that warm cockhead, he ate it, ate it like a starving man attacks a hidden cache of food. And just as his moaned started to intensify, Will sat up and leaned forward and shot his dick deeper into Tom's mouth.

Oh yeah! was Tom's only thought as the feel of it filled his world. Marcus might have had the biggest cock in creation, but it just didn't fit in Tom's mouth. Will's tan cock slid right down, fitting him perfectly, the head bumping gently into the back of his throat, the length filling his mouth, a pile of short hairs grinding against his lips and nose. He breathed in, a sharp intake of breath, and then sealed his mouth around the cock and sucked.

"Not bad, Blondie ... keep sucking, don't stop, take it all, take all you want.... In a minute, I get what I want." Will took hold of Tom's head, gently, in one hand and then took another drink. Slowly, he began to shift his hips, teasing Tom's mouth with the slightest movement of that splendid cock. Tom almost whimpered with pleasure, and sucked as though his life depended on it.

He was so intensely involved in sucking that he didn't realize anything about the passage of time. All he knew was that there was a cock in his mouth that was perfect for him. When Will pulled his head away, he actually made a sound, halfway between a sigh and a whimper, and he looked up to find out what was wrong.

Will was standing up. "I wanna plug your ass, Blondie. I wanna shoot my cum so deep in you you feel it splashing in your head. Now, do you want that, or do you want me to finish in your mouth?" Will massaged his dick while he spoke. His voice seemed deeper, hoarser.

"I ... I ..." Tom stammered, unable to think, unable to decide. In his mouth, oh, that would be glorious, to feel the cum rushing through the shaft, to hold onto him while he pulsed his pleasure! But he hadn't had a dick in his ass for months, and oh, God, he needed it! He blushed and choked, and Will grinned.

"I guess it's my choice then, Blondie. Get your buns over there, and get your pants down." He pointed to a screened-off corner, and Tom went, like a dog after a thrown toy. Behind the screen was a large, inviting bed, the covers rumpled, pillows everywhere. He heard Will following him, and without looking back, he unfastened his jeans and dropped them. He was about to kick off his sneakers when Will came up behind him and pushed him forward, so that he fell onto the bed.

"Just bend over, Blondie. I hope you're hot and open, because my dick wants to tear its way through you, man." The sound of his voice sent erotic lightning bolts through Tom's body, and his cock stiffened against the softness of the bed. His jeans held his legs together at the calf, but Will stepped up close, and tugged on the back of his shirt.

"Get your ass up here! You want it, don't you, Blondie?"

"God, yes! Fuck me, Will, fuck me. I want it!" Tom's voice was almost cracking with anticipation, and he pushed his ass up, so he was kneeling on the bed. His cock hung down, stiff and almost painful, but he didn't care.

Something cool touched his waiting asshole, and he sighed as lube was pushed into him. "That's right, nice and open, make room for daddy to come in, Blondie." A crackling sound, a wonderful, welcome crackling sound, and then the feel of pressure against that tight hole. How many months had it been since Scott had reamed out that hole?

The pressure increased, and then that familiar half-tearing, half-exploding sensation as the cock made it in and slid forward! Tom cried out his pleasure, and his cry called Will forward. With one thrust, the Latin man drove his cock deep into Tom's waiting asshole, burying it to the root!

"Oh yeah!" Tom shouted, as Will slammed into him. "Oh, yeah, fuck me, please, fuck me, oh God!"

"That's what I'm doing, Blondie ... you feel it? You like it?"

Like it? Tom was in heaven. He arched his

119

back and thrust backward to meet every new forward thrust, and he drank in every sensation offered him. Everything was right, the taste in his mouth, the dark masculinity of this shadowed sleeping place, the feel of the bed under him and the roughness of Will's fucking ... everything! Will hadn't bothered to take his jeans off, and the denim and steel buttons rubbed and bumped against Tom's ass delightfully. Even the fact that they were both mostly dressed was wonderful, everything had happened so fast! He moaned and gasped, urging Will on, and Will responded by slowing down.

"I'm not here for you now, Blondie. This is for me, got that? I cum when I want to. You just take it. And take it!"

Slowly, Will eased his cock almost all the way out of Tom's asshole, and then even more slowly slid it back in. He did this several times, and Tom's cries turned into whimpers of pleasure and need.

"Yeah, that's better. You know how to act right, Blondie. You know how to take what your man wants to give, don't you?" Will continued his erotic tease, stroking Tom's ass from time to time.

"Yeah, please, oh God ..." Tom barely knew what he was saying or whether he was supposed to answer. He just knew he never wanted this to stop!

"Well, maybe, since this is your first time, I should, you know, give you something back...." With that, Will reached around, underneath, and gripped Tom's cock in one hand, pushing his own cock forward, back into Tom's asshole. Tom shuddered and to his horror, his balls tightened and he

came! That was all it took! Just the feel of Will's
hand, and the feel of his cock, and Tom shot off a
load of cum! He voiced his frustration, and his
asshole tightened around Will's cock in orgasmic
convulsions. Will gasped himself, and began
thrusting harder again.

"You little fucker, you should never do that!"
Will cursed, beginning to fuck with an almost
angry attitude. "You little asshole, I'm gonna
ream your fucking white ass whether you like it
or not, and if you don't like it, it's your own fucking fault!"

Tom cried out again as that relentless pumping
started, and he felt how tight his asshole suddenly felt. But Will kept his promise and fucked and
pumped, until finally, he made a small cry of his
own and came, slamming into Tom's ass with a
growl.

He stood behind him for a moment, and Tom
felt Will's cock grow soft in his ass. He panted and
tried to take deeper breaths and calm down, and
when Will pulled his cock out, he whimpered and
fell forward, his belly in a pool of his own cum.
Dimly, he heard Will stripping the scumbag off.

"If you cum first, you idiot, your asshole gets
tighter. Didn't you know that?"

Tom raised his head. "Scott never told me why
..."

"Shit, you only had one other guy before me?"
Will walked around to the head of the bed and sat
down. His cock was hanging limply out of his
open fly, and he had taken his shirt off as well.

Tom shrugged. "Well, there was Marcus."

"That doesn't count. Well, what do you know?
You're practically a virgin." He grinned.

"No I'm not! Scott and me, we did lots of stuff!" Tom protested. He was still not interested in getting up, but he pushed himself up and fumbled with his pants.

"Yeah, well, you're still practically a virgin around here, Blondie. Why don't you strip down the rest of the way. I may want to fuck you again."

Tom stopped and looked up at Will. The Latino's eyes were shining in the dim light. "Yeah, I mean it, Blondie. You may be one sorry virgin shithead, but you're cute. Stick around, and I'll start your real education, man. Teach you things that count in this world. And between the two of us, man, we make up for that asshole Marcus, you know? For a while." And Will leaned over and kissed Tom, gently, on the mouth. "But first, go get a fucking towel and clean up your mess, man. Shit, I hate wet beds."

CHAPTER SIX

VI.

It was a blissful weekend. Will ended up taking
Tom to get some new clothes and those new
sneakers he wanted, and then took him out to a
gay club where they danced. Tom watched envi-
ously as Will took his shirt off on the dance floor
and moved to the whistles and admiring calls of
the men surrounding them, but then Will took
him home and fucked him silly all over again.
And this time, Tom contained his cum until it was
the right time.

It was like a miracle, watching the young
Hispanic move, gazing at his beautiful body, and
then being the recipient of his lustful attentions.
With his sculpted body, dark features and pan-
therlike walk, he was sexuality incarnate. When

they made love the second time, deep into the night, Tom explored every inch of Will's body, covering it with his worshipful kisses. He could scarcely believe what he was experiencing. It was a real dream come true. He slept, cradled in Will's arms, with a slight smile on his lips.

On Sunday morning, Will sent Tom home, and Tom didn't ask about what Will had to do that day. But they spoke on the phone in the afternoon, and again that night, and Tom felt a warm sensation grow between them. For all his tough words, Will seemed to really like him. And they had a shared experience that bound them together, even if they didn't mention it again.

In that well-used bed on Saturday night, Tom told Will his own life story, talking about Scott and his parents, and being lonely, and felt much better after it was all out. And while he did his laundry at the corner laundromat on Sunday, he realized that not being alone was one of the most important things about knowing Will, about fucking with him. He took the money he had put aside for a neighborhood hustler's attentions, and spent it on a radio and a new set of sheets.

But Monday morning arrived, and with it came a feeling that Tom recognized from school. It was deep down, in the pit of his stomach, a need to stay home and bury his head under the covers, and just not go out that day. But fear of what might happen if he didn't show up won him over, and he dressed and walked down to the gym.

His new sneakers squeaked against the tiles that he mopped. But everything was in its place, everyone was doing what they came to do, and it was just like any other day at the gym. A note from the weekend manager, Larry, told him that the juice machine was broken, and he called the repair company to come down and fix it. He reported this to Frank Dobbs, who acknowledged it with a grunt and sent him back to work without comment.

All in all, it seemed a normal day. Nothing different about it at all. He took a long lunch at Alex's suggestion when he was told that there was some work to be done after 5 PM, but there was nothing special about that. He had been warned that he would be staying late quite a bit, and he had accepted that.

When he came back from lunch, he found an envelope and a bottle of vitamins in his locker. He opened the envelope and glanced through the contents, his lunch suddenly heavy in his gut. It was a workout regimen, complete with dietary suggestions and guidelines and an progressive chart showing when and how to intensify the exercises. The starting date was today ... and it had been circled. He pushed the envelope back into the locker and closed the metal door, as though it would lock away the memories of his experience last week. He went back to work, slightly dazed, and tried to concentrate on his job.

How can he expect me to follow all of that and do my job, he asked himself as he picked up a basket of used towels. I have a lot of shit to do here! And Alex wants me to stay late, too. I have to talk to him, explain to him, tell him I can't, I'm really not up to it; maybe he'll call me a wimp and just let me go.

That thought made him stop. Would that work? If he really just wimped out? Showed no poten-

tial? The image that came to his mind was so
repulsive and personally humiliating that he
blushed, and had to throw himself into his work
to hide it. Besides, he thought, soberly, if he didn't
get turned off by my fucking begging him not to
hurt me, he won't fall for that, either.

What a dilemma! If it wasn't one thing, it was
another. Yeah, he wanted to build up, he wanted
the companionship of strong, masculine men, but
not like this! Maybe he'll get bored real quick, he
thought (or hoped). Maybe he'll find someone else.
(And do the same to them? You are one cowardly
piece of shit, Tom Kake, one sorry sonofabitch.
You'd wish this on someone else to spare your ass,
wouldn't you?)

That made him feel bad for a long time, until
he realized it wasn't really true. I don't want anyone to have to go through this, he said to himself.
But I don't know how to stop it from happening to
me, let alone anyone else.

At five o'clock, the night shift started to come
in, and Alex told him to straighten up one of the
private rooms, that it had been used heavily all
day. It was true, the lights had always been on at
one time or another. Tom took his cleaning sup-
plies into the room and sighed in exasperation. It
was a mess!

There were towels hanging from the equipment
and bunched up in wet bundles on the floor and
mats. Several mats were tossed together in a pile,
with tension bands for the resistance machine
scattered among them. The whole room smelled of
heavy, sour sweat, wet and thick.

Tom switched the exhaust fan on and started
work. First, he picked up the mats and hung

128

them up, except for the damp one, which he spread out to dry. The towels he threw into an empty bucket, and then he started putting the equipment back where it belonged, sorting bands and extra parts and lining them up properly. He cleaned, disinfected and then polished the actual equipment, the bench and the resistance machine, and then treated the chin-up and sit-up bars to a polish as well. By the time he was finished, it looked like a new place, clean and bright, smelling slightly of bleach and slightly of lemon, and only faintly of old sweat. With a heavy sigh, he prepared to leave.

Then, the door opened and Frank Dobbs walked in. He was wearing sweats and a gym T-shirt with the sleeves hacked off, and he had his weight lifters' belt on. He was carrying an envelope.

"Good job, Tommy, nice job. You got everything nice and clean," he said, his ugly face cracking into a smile.

Tom eyed the envelope with horror. He was sure it was the same one that had been in his locker. He looked up and said, "Uh, thanks, Mr. Dobbs ... um, I gotta ... I'm kind of late...."

"Yeah, for your first work out. Mr. Marcus told me." Frank shook the envelope and then took the contents out. "He's busy, so I'm gonna test you out and see what you're made of. You brought work-out clothes?"

"Uh, no!" Tom grasped the chance. "I ... I have to go get some. Can we start tomorrow?"

"Nah, I don't think so." Frank's grin got even wider. "Me and Mr. Marcus, we always figured, you don't need real special clothes to work out in.

Besides, this isn't gonna be a full session, only a whatdoyoucallit, a test. I gotta see what you can do and tell Mr. Marcus, so's he can adjust your program. Strip down, those jeans ain't gonna work for this."

Tom's mouth went dry. "Mr. Dobbs, can't this wait until tomorrow? I've had a real long day...." To his horror, he realized that he was sounding like the man who Frank had so abused in the private shower room, and he swallowed hard.

"Do it, shitface. Now. You gotta learn, you can't walk out on a deal with Mr. Marcus, boy. Yeah, he told me. He tells me everything, asshole, everything. So get those fucking pants off, and let's get going, because I don't have all fucking night!"

Tom kicked his sneakers off and slid his pants down his legs. He had remembered Marcus' admonition not to wear jockeys, so he had a brand new jockstrap on, wrapping his cock and balls up on a round package between his legs. He dropped the pants on top of the shoes.

"Yeah, might as well take the shirt off too. I wanna see all of you, see what we need to do to make you a man." Frank's tone was heavy with sarcasm, and Tom silently stripped off his sweaty T-shirt.

"You're too fucking skinny," was Frank's first pronouncement. "You got no tone, no build. Look at you! You're arms are soft, no muscle, you're even starting to have a little belly there. Shit, and what are you, twenty?"

"I'm almost twenty-one," Tom muttered.

"Yeah? Well, almost doesn't count, asshole. This ain't a game of horseshoes here." Frank came closer and poked at him. "Shit, almost twenty-one, huh? And already you're going to pot. Well, we're gonna stop that right fuckin' now. Didja read the stuff about what you're supposed to eat and shit?"

"Yeah ... but I don't know a lot of that stuff, I don't know where to get it, what to do. You gotta give me some time to get used to it...."

"Oh, give me a motherfucking break!" Frank yelled into Tom's face. "Are you a man under there, or are you some kinda shivering little boy? You don't know how to do something, you fucking ask, asshole! You don't know where to get something, you fucking ask! I know you came from Dogshit, Nebraska, but you can't be *that* ignorant!" He pulled back and pointed to the mat on the floor. "Go stand over there, and try not to look too goddamn stupid!"

Tom did as he was told, and stood still while Frank measured his arms and legs and waist and chest and jotted numbers down in a little book he took out of his pocket. "You're too fucking skinny," he repeated, with each measure. And next to his massive, knotted muscles, Tom could see why the man would think so.

"OK. Mr. Marcus says you gotta start with your arms, chest, and stomach. You're probably gonna start out light, 'cause you're not eating right, but as soon as you get with the program, we'll speed you up. You're gonna be into some heavy duty cross-training real soon, so pay attention! You got so little fucking raw material, it's like starting from nothing. Get your ass down and give me fifty push-ups."

He backed away again, and Tom lowered himself to the floor. It was a long time since he did push-ups regularly, and his arms and back told him so. At his internal count of thirty, he began to feel slightly tired, but he pushed his way to fifty and got up.

"That was so fucking pathetic, I can't stand it," Frank said, his voice hard. "You can't even do fifty fucking push-ups without losing your wind. On your back, you fucking wimp, let's see fifty sit-ups!"

The sit-ups were harder, and Tom had to deal with Frank screaming in his ear through the last ten. "What the fuck's the matter with you, you fucking pantywaist? Any middle-aged bastard that comes here can do this! Shit, you should be starting every day with 150 of each, you sorry excuse for a swinging dick!"

Somehow, Tom got through them, and sweat began to gather under his arms and across his chest and along his neck. When he was finished, Frank pointed toward the resistance machine, and told him how to set it up. He endured at least ten different sets of exercises, pushing against the tension bands with his arms and his chest, with his legs, with his entire body. He began to hurt, a familiar hurt, one he had almost forgotten; and each time he slowed down, Frank was in his ear, screaming curses and commands, calling him names and deriding his manhood. It scared him, but Frank's words were far preferable to his potential for physical abuse, so Tom kept his mouth shut and kept trying, kept lifting and pressing, and sweating.

"Oh, you are such a sorry fucking specimen, I don't know what the fuck to tell Mr. Marcus. You are one pathetic piece of shit, let me tell you,

Tommy boy." Frank made a few more notes in his little book as Tom leaned over an arm of the machine and panted. "You can't even do a series of simple reps that any little kid can do, shit, that my grandfather could probably do. Mr. Marcus was absolutely right, asshole. You need discipline. 'Cause you got none. Now before you're outa here tonight, you're gonna do all those things all over again, asshole, from the beginning."

Tom looked up in sheer disbelief. "I can't!" he blurted out. "I ... I can barely catch my breath! It's not healthy to overwork.... It's been a long time since I worked out.... I should start slower...."

Frank's face became a mask of disbelief itself, and his squinty eyes widened in surprise. "And who the fuck are you to tell me what's healthy or not, you little asswipe? You think you know better then me? You think you know better than Mr. Marcus what's good for you and what's not? Well, lemme tell you something, asshole, you *never* tell me what's right, and what you can't do! You do every fucking thing I tell you to, and if you drop stone dead, it's your own damn fucking fault, do you understand? Hit the floor! We're starting over, and you're not gonna be finished until you do everything I tell you to!"

Tom dripped sweat onto the mat when he went down, but he pushed himself into position and started the rise and fall of push-ups once again. At twenty-three, he began to falter, and then, he felt an explosion of pain along his ass.

"Ow!" he exclaimed, falling forward.

The belt followed him. Frank raised and lowered his arm five more times, putting five red stripes across Tom's ass while he writhed in pain on the mat. Then, he stopped.

"Now, you get that ass back up, boy. And you keep going. Because every time you stop, you're gonna get the same. Now git!"

Tom struggled up and down, and cursed endlessly, and sweated and hurt. And when he was finished, it was over on his back, and the belt was slapping his chest and stomach and thighs, until they were as striped as his ass. His body became tender over every square inch, and he began to grunt in pain with every new slash of the belt. But he couldn't decide what was worse, the belt or the reps.

And Frank never stopped. He never stopped yelling, never stopped driving him forward, and that belt was always ready to rise when Tom stopped to breathe or rest. It was finally on the machine where Frank misjudged on his aim and the edge of that wide belt smacked that white bundle between Tom's legs.

Tom screamed, dropped the bars, and doubled forward instinctively. "Oh, Jesus! Oh God, my nuts, oh, Jesus!"

"Fuckin' wimp," Frank said. "Can't even take a shot to the balls without cryin' like a goddamn baby. I think I've had enough of watching you trying to act like a man, asshole." He walked over to the wretched young man and physically pulled him up, off the bench, and then dragged him toward the door.

Tom felt the pain still shooting through him. He didn't even try to resist as Frank "helped" him into the hallway and past the free-weight room. No one noticed them, or at least no one who said anything. Frank led him downstairs, and it wasn't until Tom realized that they were heading toward the private showers that he began to struggle. Frank didn't even seem to notice.

Instead, he propelled Tom into the room, and Tom hit the floor and rolled over to protect his already bruised cock and balls.

"You wait here, asshole. No, you won't do that, will you? Let's see if I can impress on you the need to stay put." Frank opened a locker and pulled out a pair of handcuffs and snapped them open, the ratchet sound echoing in the small room.

Tom tried to pull away, but Frank was on top of him in a second, locking the cuffs on one wrist. Then, the large, ugly man pulled Tom over to the row of urinals and handcuffed him to one of the pipes. The smell of chlorine and old piss filled Tom's world, and he sank down against the cold tile wall.

"There. Now, you'll stay put. And do me a favor, asshole, think about just what I can do to you if I want to. It'll make you want to be smarter. You can't get much dumber!" Laughing at his own observations, Frank left the room.

Oh God, what was going to be next, Tom thought, cupping his balls gently. Haven't I done enough? Hasn't he? But inside, he knew that his first workout at the gym wasn't going to be over until Frank shot his load, somewhere. But what had he gone to get? Or do? Or say? Did he go to report to Mr. Marcus? Did he go to get some coffee? Tom almost laughed, but swallowed it and shivered against the tiles. I'm going nuts already, he thought. Oh, God, I hurt, every part of my body hurts, and what kind of a man would do that to another man? It was inconceivable.

It hurt.

When the door opened, he expected to see Frank or Marcus, and was genuinely shocked when Alex walked in. He pulled himself closer to the wall, and couldn't even think to speak, but Alex didn't look surprised to see him. Instead, the manager reached into his sweatpants and pulled them down to reveal a cock that was already stiff.

"So, looks like Frank got you all wrapped up," the man said, coming closer. "Looks like he worked you over a little too."

Oh shit, Tom thought. What did Will say? They were all once Marcus' toys. Now, they're his ... bullies. He clenched his teeth as Alex stepped closer.

"Let me get a feel before Frank gets back. Open up, Tommy." Alex pulled Tom up to crotch level by his hair and thrust his cock toward and into Tom's mouth. He thrust in and out a few times, and then pulled out and slapped Tom across the face. "Come on, don't just take it, suck it."

And Tom did, closing his eyes in resignation. He opened them again when he heard the door open again, and his heart sank when he saw that it was Larry, the night maintenance man, and John, the other manager. They were followed by Frank, who was grinning again.

"Hey, what's the deal, Al, you started early?" Larry joked, closing in on the scene.

"Yeah, well, the early bird gets the cocksucker, you know?"

There was laughter, rough, masculine laughter, and Tom choked on the dick in his mouth.

"You didn't know, did you, asshole?" Frank asked, watching Alex fuck Tom's face. "Yeah, we're all in this together. And these fine men have all gone through a training program just like the one you're starting. And they loved it so fucking much, they're gonna help you out with yours. You should thank 'em. Is he thankin' you, Al?"

"Oh yeah!" Alex slammed his cock into Tom's throat several times. "Yeah, he's thanking me real nice!"

"Well, don't hog the thanks, Al. Let someone else get thanked, too!" Frank pulled Alex away, but the man didn't protest. And before he could draw a decent breath, Tom's mouth was filled by Larry's stiffening cock, which slammed its way down where Al recently was.

"Shit, he says 'thank you' in a way I like!" Larry said, getting in a few good thrusts before Frank tapped him out. And Tom was compelled to take a third cock down his throat as well, and he was left feeling dizzy and bruised, handcuffed to a cold piss pipe, as the three men backed off and waited for instructions from Frank.

"Now, this is Mr. Marcus' new boy," Frank said, pointing toward him. "His name is Tommy. Say hello to Tommy, guys."

"Hello, Tommy!"

"Nice cocksucking, Tommy."

"Hiya, asshole!"

Tom hung his head. He couldn't bear to watch them standing in front of him, cocks hanging out, hunger in their eyes.

"He's also Mr. Marcus' new toy, so don't be playing with him without permission. We got special permission tonight. Mr. Marcus wants this shithead to understand what his place is around here. Look at me, shithead!"

Tom looked up, miserable.

"You are the lowest of the low, asshole. Any guy in this place is better then you, any fucking one. You belong to Mr. Marcus now, body and soul. Do you understand that, cocksucker?"

Tom nodded.

"Then say it!"

"I ... I belong to Mr. Marcus."

"And say that you're an asshole."

"An-and I'm, an a-asshole."

The men laughed again.

"Well, I'm glad you know that, asshole, I surely am glad. 'Cause knowing that is your first step toward becoming a man, isn't it, guys?" They agreed, laughing and grinning and holding onto their cocks. "And all these guys wanna help you get out of that asshole status, don't they?"

"Yeah, eventually!" said Larry. "After he learns his manners!"

"Yeah, we're all gonna help you become a man, asshole. But first, you gotta learn what it's like not being one." Frank leaned over and unlocked the cuff attaching Tom to the urinal, and then pulled him up. Turning him around, he locked both of Tom's wrists behind his back and pushed him into the waiting arms of the other three men.

They caught him effortlessly, and fell immediately to exploring his body. Hands ran all over him, squeezing his jock, spreading his cheeks, pinching his nipples, slapping his ass ... fingers invaded him, exploring his mouth and ass, and he cried out.

"What a baby," one of them said.

"Here, give the baby something to suck!"

He was pushed into a chest, his mouth against a nipple, and he sucked for a while. The men behind him slapped his ass over and over again, and he moaned, and he was dragged from one chest to another.

"Shit, he's not bad," Larry said, arching his back.

"Yes he is. We shouldn't let him on his feet among men." Frank's hands pushed Tom down onto his knees, and a cock immediately slid into his mouth. He heard Frank say to someone, "Get me hard," and he shivered. The man whose cock he was sucking ... was it Alex? grabbed hold of his head and roughly fucked his face.

"How do you want him?" Alex asked, grinding his cock into Tom.

"Here. Put these under his ass, get him on his back. You guys can take turns on his face while I break him in."

"Yeah!"

"OK ... let's do it!"

Tom was manipulated down on his back, a pile of something soft under the base of his spine, his wrists pressed into the tile floor. From this new position, everyone looked like giants, huge, horny giants looking over their captive. They stripped off the rest of their clothing and stood, all marvelous specimens of manhood, all showing the effects of a dedicated program of training. Tom swallowed hard. In any other circumstance, this would be a wet dream. But instead, he was cold, and sore, and they were looking down at him like they were ready to dissect him. He decided not to waste any more breath trying to talk his way out.

Frank was getting a blowjob from John as Alex and Larry lowered Tom to the floor and positioned him. "Yeah, that's it," he said, nodding. "Al, you come over here and grab a leg. John, feed him your cock for a while. You, get this on me, that's it, use your mouth, like I taught you, yeah, that's nice. Get it on nice and tight and leave a little spit there. But just a little ... we want him to feel this, don't we? Good. Now, grab his other leg. We're gonna open this asshole up."

John settled down over Tom's head and did as Frank told him to do. Tom opened his mouth submissively and let the man plow his way in, although the position was uncomfortable. He was much more concerned with the way Al grabbed hold of one leg and lifted it up, pulling Tom's ass up in the air. In a moment, there was another strong hand on his other leg, and carefully, they were pulled apart. His asscheeks separated, and he gulped around the cock in his mouth as Frank's large, crooked dick thrust into his exposed asshole without warning.

"Oh, shit, this kid is tight!" Frank exclaimed. "Shit! Almost tight as a virgin!"

"Then you're doing him a favor, Frank," Larry offered. "If the boss was at him first, he'd be in the hospital!"

"Yeah," Frank responded, enjoying the feeling. "Yeah, I'm doin' him a favor!"

Tom was overwhelmed. Between the cock in his mouth and the one plowing his ass, he just couldn't cope! He choked several times, and John pulled out. "He's almost useless on this end! You're distracting him, Frank!"

"Well, switch with Larry!" Frank shoved his dick in tight and grunted. Tom groaned at the intrusion. "See if he gets better service!"

The switch was done, and the awful attack continued. Frank did not seem to be in a rush to cum, and he orchestrated the gang bang, changing the cock or balls that went into Tom's mouth as it suited him. The lack of lubrication on his dick made every thrust a sharp, painful intrusion, and Tom made muffled cries around the various cocks and balls that were dipped into his mouth. The men laughed at him when they weren't concentrating on their own pleasure, and Frank in particular had a great time. Every once in a while, he would pull all the way back, leaving just the head of his cock inside of Tom, and then slam it back in to the root, slapping Tom's asscheeks at the same time.

Finally, he yelled, "Back off! Everyone back off ... let's do it!" And instantly, the hands holding Tom's legs vanished, and Frank took them into his own hands, pulling Tom's ass up to meet his cock. Alex, whose cock was back in Tom's mouth, got up, and the three men stood over him as Frank pounded his cock into his asshole. All three of them started working their own dicks.

"Yeah, that's it, gonna fuck your ass, rip you up, take it, asshole, you new fucking toy, take it all ... OK, guys, let him have it!"

Larry was the first. His hand was a blur on his dick, and his cum shot out in ropes of thick, white goo, splattering across Tom's chest. Alex groaned and added his own, hitting Tom across the belly and splashing against his jock. Then John leaned forward and shot a load up against his neck and chin.

141

Frank came last, but he came big. Growling and snarling, he wrenched his dick back and forth, in and out, holding Tom's body in his arms, until he shot. Tom could swear that he could feel the heat of Frank's cum like a jet of hot water filling the scumbag. And Frank didn't stop at once. He kept pounding forward, squeezing the last drop of juice out of his dick, and then he reached forward and jerked Tom's jock down. His hardened hand wrapped around Tom's cock and pulled at it.

"Now you're gonna shoot, asshole. This is your first time, you get to shoot. And if you don't, we got all night to make you, got that? Oh, yeah, he's nice and hard, he loved every fucking minute of it, didn't he? He just loves to have dicks shoved in his body, loves to feel cum all over his scummy body...."

Tom shook and groaned, and against his will, his cock rose under Frank's words and his hard hand. He gasped and arched his back, and sure enough, his own cum spurted out, covering Frank's hand, spilling back to cover his own shaft and balls. He cried out at the unfairness of it all.

Frank abruptly pulled out of Tom's ass and stripped the condom off. Just as he did with the man on Friday morning, he spilled the contents out onto Tom's body. Then, he got up.

"Here, take the cuffs off him and bring him into the shower. He stinks."

Hands turned him over and he groaned at the rush of blood to his hands. The cuffs were removed, and he was pulled to his feet. His entire body ached, and his arms trembled with the return of sensation. They pulled and pushed him

142

into the small shower room, and then unceremoniously dropped him to the tile floor, near a drain.

"Welcome to the gym," Frank said, fingering his softened dick. It was still monstrously ugly. "Now that you passed the initiation, you get baptized."

Tom opened his mouth to protest, and then closed it immediately as Frank began to piss. He closed his eyes and tried to back away, pushing himself against the wall, covering his head with his arms. The other men joined in, and their hot showers covered his body and filled him with shame. They laughed as they emptied themselves on and at him, and then began to leave. Before letting the door close behind him, Frank called out, "And clean this place up, asshole! It smells like cum and piss!"

It was very late when Tom left the gym. The envelope was waiting for him by the door, and he took it.

CHAPTER SEVEN

VII.

Three Months Later.

"Hey, you're starting to shape up, Tom!" Mike said, as Tom passed him two towels. "You're really looking good these days, nice haircut, nice clothes. Nice tan, too."

Tom smiled. The tan did suit him, he had to admit. Especially now, in the middle of winter, when everyone else seemed so pale. But he didn't know about the shaping up part. No matter how hard he worked, no matter how far he progressed, he was nowhere near anything noticeable. At least, not to his eyes. Or Mr. Marcus'. It was Marcus who sent him to a tanning booth twice a week, Marcus who told him where to go to get his hair cut, what foods to eat, and what to avoid. On some days, Tom found himself wondering when he would need Marcus to tell him how to breathe. But all of the man's directions seemed to be taking Tom to where he would have wanted to go. He was filling out, and getting stronger, and his body was becoming more attractive. But not nearly as attractive as Marcus wanted it to be, and not as quickly as he demanded it must be.

"Thanks, Mike," he said. "I keep trying. It'll be a while before I get to looking like you guys, though."

"Ha, what a kidder. With those big baby blues, you're already a killer, Tom, take my word for it. And trust me, you're really shaping up. Couple of months, and you're gonna leave us far behind." He stripped off his shirt, and Tom smiled at the sight of his pierced nipples. He had gotten used to seeing all sorts of piercings, tattoos, and assorted strange body decorations in his months at the gym.

"Besides, I hear Marcus thinks you can compete one of these days. If you can, you'll be bound to win. No one Marcus has ever trained turned out to be a loser. You lucked out here, Tom."

"Uh, yeah." Tom turned away quickly and went back to his cart. He moved easily, and there was no way that Mike could possibly know that Tom's ass and legs were a mass of bruises, bad enough to keep them covered for the rest of the week. He had grown accustomed to the pain.

Because the pain never stopped, at least not during his work week. Every Tuesday and every Friday, he had a private training session with either Frank or Mr. Marcus himself. And every session included some form of physical discipline and some form of sexual use. And as time passed, the two men seemed to grow more inventively cruel. Despite the way he looked and the money he had saved, despite the friends he had and his fabulous lover, he was living in hell. Every happy moment he had was contrasted to the eventual return to some hot, sweaty room, and the twisted uses and commands of a pair of torturers.

Marcus had looked at the report that Frank Dobbs gave him after the "initiation night," and had adjusted Tom's program a bit. But essentially, it was almost inhumanly brutal. Tom worked out every morning, and once more every night. He was not allowed to really recover from his beatings, and sometimes the agony of sitting on a bench the next day was worse then the actual beating itself. They were both very careful not to *really* hurt him. They concentrated on his ass, his shoulders, and sometimes on his legs, when they used belts. They almost never struck his mouth, or his face, although he had fallen many times into walls, fixtures, and machines.

But it was the more *inventive* things they did that kept getting to him. He was almost used to getting beaten. But those other things ...

When Marcus decided that Tom needed more inspiration when bench-pressing, he brought in a small device that looked like something you would connect a radio with, or use to conduct some kind of experiment. It rapidly became one of Tom's most hated "training aids."

He had been lying on his back, already tired from earlier exercises, and his arms just didn't seem capable of doing even one complete rep of lifts. Marcus had looked at him for a moment, left the room, and then c0me back a few minutes later. Tom had known better than to leave while Marcus was gone.

The gym owner arrived with a contraption that looked like a new addition to the weight machine. He spent a moment rigging it, and Tom gazed at what looked like a fishing weight, dangling above his head. Two cords dropped down on his chest, and he blanched when he saw what they were ... two little metal clips, with saw-tooth edges.

"You don't seem to understand how important it is for you to work those arms and that chest, boy. Maybe this will remind you." Marcus then handcuffed Tom's wrists to the lifting handle, and reached down to open the clips. Tom almost screamed when they closed on each nipple, but he strangled the cry back.

What made it worse was the weight! It was a fishing weight, a little black diamond of metal, and as long as Tom's arms (and the bar) were down, it hung free, tugging on his sore nipples. When he raised the bar, it released the tension on the cords, and his nipples, still stinging from the clips, were temporarily relieved of the weight.

Those little weights became a nightmare to Tom. Every time they came out, he was in for some kind of exotic pain. They appeared when he did squats, attached by those evil little clips to the flesh on his cock and balls. They came back to his nipples for push-ups and pull-ups. The clips by themselves were occasionally used for what Marcus called "come-alongs," little leashes to encourage faster or more regular moves. Tom's nipples were perpetually sore and scabbed. They had gotten a little tougher so far, but not nearly enough.

He was lucky that Marcus did think of putting him in competition. Otherwise, Tom knew that he might be sporting rings in those nipples, and God knows how tragic that might turn out to be.

The sexual uses continued as well, and Tom was now quite intimately acquainted with Frank's crooked cock and Marcus' machine. It had taken him almost two months to be able to take the machine into his throat, and when he did, it usually left him sore and hoarse for days. For a while, Marcus had him coming to his office first thing every morning and taking as much as he could, for fifteen or twenty minutes. He would laugh, and remind Tom that training was a universal concept, and threaten him with ass-fucking if he didn't learn to take the machine properly.

It had been a very good threat. Tom had begged like he'd never thought he could, begged as though his very life was in danger, and amazingly, Marcus had agreed. Tom's ass, according to Frank, was just too tight to take Marcus' cock without sustaining damage. So he started yet another training program, which Tom hated as much as he did the nipple clips and weights.

That one started one night after Frank had just finished vigorously fucking him. He was tied, for convenience, over a bench in an otherwise empty weight room, his body streaked with sweat and striped with reddened lines of abuse. Frank liked tying him up, liked having him absolutely still while he plowed his way into one end or another. But as he lay there panting, expecting Frank to untie him, he felt something new getting shoved into his ass, being twisted and pushed in with violent strength. He cried out in pain.

"Aw, you're such a fucking baby, Tommy. This here is good for you! The boss says we gotta open your tight ass up, and that's what we're gonna do." With a savage twist, the thing was pushed all the way in. Tom felt like he was stuffed with a watermelon. It burned, and he twisted and strained against his ropes.

"Yeah, that's good. We'll leave that in for a while, and then you can wear it home. And it better be up there when you come in tomorrow morning, cocksucker ... and speaking of that ..."

Frank came around to the front to take advantage of the only hole left.

When Tom got home and pulled the hateful thing out, he gasped at the size of it. It was a butt plug, a huge one, and fat. It had a fat base and a little flange on the end to keep it from going all the way in, but Tom was amazed that it got in at all. His butt still hurt on the morning, but he bit back tears and managed to get it back in, with the help of lots of lube. It was a good thing, too. As soon as he got in, Marcus sent for him, had him take down his pants and show him the plug. Tom was then rewarded by a half hour session sucking on the machine, while Marcus told him how interesting it was going to be when Tom was open enough for Marcus to fuck him properly.

The plugs became a part of Tom's life, and he was forced to wear them during his normal working hours, and occasionally through his workouts. Frank particularly liked to see Tom on a rowing machine with a plug buried up his ass. The movements and the pressure made it almost seem like he was being impaled with every stroke. Sometimes, Frank would stand at the front of the machine, and whenever Tom pulled himself forward, he would open his lips and take in a mouthful of ugly cock. One night, with the tit-clamps held in Frank's hand and a huge plug up his ass, every backward stroke became a scream muffled by a mouthful of dick on every forward stroke. Frank came three times that night.

Will's description of Marcus being the brains and Frank the enforcer turned out to be very true. Frank was brutal, yes, and he was a harsh taskmaster, but Marcus was the creative one. He was also sexually insatiable. He could leave one private session and go directly to another and the machine would rise to the occasion. There was no time when Marcus couldn't get it up, and to Tom's fevered imagination, Marcus seemed to have a perpetual erection. It demanded worship, and much to his own personal shame, Tom was always overwhelmed with desire and weakness when he saw it.

That was one other aspect of hell. Though as much as he hated it, the constant pain and humiliation, the force and the blackmail, he seemed to forget all that when that machine loomed over his face. It bathed him in cum in real life and in his dreams, and nothing he could do seemed to break him of that.

Will Rodriguez was almost his savior these days. He magically took Tom away from the world in the gym and swept him into a world of exciting nightlife and pleasurable afternoons. The city-bred man took the country mouse under one arm and taught him important things about living in the city, where to eat and shop, and how to read the subway map. On warmer days, they went to

parks and watched boys playing football and soc-
cer, and on colder days they went to movies. Tom
met a lot of Will's "friends," and learned to stop
blushing when they told him how hot the two of
them looked together, and would they consider
doing a threesome? For some reason, Tom just
couldn't. Will never asked why or pushed, and
Tom left him alone when he needed to see one of
his "friends."

Will came over to Tom's dreary apartment and
shook his head at the place and started to help to
spruce it up, claiming that he would never sleep
in a dump like that. So Tom's first major purchase
was a large bed, which the two of them wrestled
up the stairs one day and gleefully broke in minutes after it was in place. The faded green hospital sheets went back to Mr. D'Angelo with thanks.

Sex with Will was always great, and Tom
couldn't get enough of it. He was always ready for
him, eager to devour him with kisses, swallow
him to the root, pull open his ass cheeks to be joyfully impaled. As they spent more time together,
Will grew more likely to do fun things, like wres-
tle with him, or try strange, acrobatic positions.
They showered together until the hot water ran
out, exploring each others bodies and pleasuring
each other. They watched late-night TV and ate
Chinese food in bed and slept tangled together.

And each Monday, their little world would van-
ish, and they would be back at the gym.

Will almost never spoke of what his relationship with Marcus was like, not after that first
time. Tom never saw them together, although he
knew of Will's private sessions the same way Will
knew about his. But Tom would talk about his

experiences and feelings, and sometimes climb into Will's arms for comfort and security while Will would never say a word about what exactly was happening with him. Tom sometimes felt that he wanted to know, but mostly he didn't. The thought of knowing that Marcus treated Will the same way Tom was being treated was too much to bear.

From time to time, he looked through the want ads and tried to think of a way out of the situation, but he never could. And no matter how bad it got, the thought of his family seeing those tapes—because it was more then one tape by now—was too terrible to consider.

So he went to work every day and did his workouts and endured his training sessions and dreamed of the weekend, where he would heal enough to face Monday again.

Tom fell into the rhythm of working at the gym easily. He was always on top of things that had to be done, and he cleaned so often that complaints dropped considerably within two months. It was not too hard to be conscientious—he was liable for more punishments if he didn't take care of his work properly. After he dropped off a load of towels to the locker room, he went on his rounds and cleaned up a private room and wiped down the free-weight benches in the weight room. When he finished up in there, Alex met him at the door and hooked one thumb over his shoulder, a leer on his face.

"The boss wants to see you in his office, Tommy. Now."

Neither Alex nor the other two who had been

in on Frank's "initiation" had used Tom since. Apparently, Frank had been telling the truth about Tom being off limits, and Tom was grateful for little favors. But that didn't stop them from making gestures, slapping his ass or groping his sore tits or his cock, or from making obscene remarks in his presence. He passed Alex in the doorway and ducked down the hall, the manager's laughter echoing behind him.

He went directly into the inner office and stood inside the door. Marcus was on the phone, and when he saw Tom, he beckoned and pointed to the space on the floor between his feet. Tom went over immediately and knelt, and still talking, Marcus pulled the machine out of his pants and pulled Tom's head toward it.

Tom wet his lips and took a deep breath and inhaled the head into his mouth. He closed his eyes and began to gently suck on it and wet it down. He had learned that this lubricated it enough to help when Marcus decided to shove it into his throat. Above him, Marcus was chatting with someone.

"Huh? Oh yeah, the black kid, the one with the African name. Yeah, he's good, I'd put him in your string, he's about ready for that. The cameras like him too, he looks really good when he's oiled up. You sonofabitch, that's great news! Sure, I'm glad to hear it. The better the competition, the better my boys look when they win, right?" He laughed, and vibrations ran along the length of the machine. Tom swallowed a little more, trying to relax.

"No, no, I let that one go. He didn't listen to me, bought some steroids. I found them in his locker and kicked his ass all the way back to

Omaha, or wherever the fuck he came from. Hey, I don't care if you don't believe me. But my boys are healthy, they don't need any gunk to make them hot ... yeah, yeah ... well, speaking of hot, how was that little number I sent you a couple of months ago? Uh-huh, I thought you'd like him. No, my compliments. I have all I can get. What? Oh yeah, hell, one's trying to suck my dick right now."

Tom blushed and choked as Marcus laughed again. "Yeah, well, you know how difficult that can be, don't you? No, he's not as good as you were, but he will be. It was harder to break his ass in, too. Yeah, maybe. You let me know when you're coming in, and I'll see what I got for you. My best to the boys, ride 'em hard!" The phone came down, and Marcus grabbed Tom's head and pulled him violently down over his massive cock, impaling the young man in his lap. Tom was luck enough to catch a breath before he was jerked forward, and the machine lodged firmly in his gullet.

"Ahh, you're getting better, Tommy boy, getting better." Marcus held Tom there for a few moments, enjoying the convulsive pressure of his throat against the head of his cock. Then, he pulled him back, just as tears were forming in Tom's eyes and he was starting to get dizzy. "Get up and over this desk, boy. I think it's time for another plowing."

Tom got up and unfastened his jeans and pulled them partway down. He bent forward over the cleared desk in stoic resignation. Marcus leaned back in his chair and examined the bruises on Tom's ass and thighs, and spread his cheeks. Tom's butthole was clean.

"No plug today, boy?"

"No, Mr. Marcus ... Frank didn't say ... I mean, no one told me I should...."

"Well, I just hope you're open, boy," Marcus interrupted. "I want to shoot off in that tight ass of yours, but I better not have any trouble getting in."

"No sir, I mean, yes sir. Do you want me to get more lube?" Tom shook with tension.

"No. I've got another way to open you up." A drawer opened and then closed, and Marcus walked around to the front of the desk. He was holding a large dildo, mounted on a molded handle. It looked to be about eight or nine inches long, but it had rings of increasing sizes going down the shaft. "Open wide, Tommy, and suck this down. Just make believe that it's my cock."

Tom opened his mouth and took the dildo's head in. It tasted like old tires. Without warning, Marcus shoved it in, and Tom gagged on it, his body shaking.

"Don't you dare make a mess, boy," Marcus warned. "Just suck on this and wet it down. The wetter you get it, the easier it goes in and the less likely I'll have to take it out and put it in your mouth again." He smiled and began to make fucking motions with it, jerking it in and out of Tom's lips.

"Oh, you're coming along nicely, Tommy, very nicely. I like the way you're obeying orders these days, you're much quicker, and much more respectful. That's it, suck on that fuck-stick, get it all wet." Marcus stroked the machine absently. "And you're sticking to the program too. It shows. You're still a worthless punk, but you're starting to shape up. Maybe soon, I'll give you someone to fuck, although who would enjoy that pathetic dick of yours, I don't know. That's one thing we can't improve on you, my little cocksucker. You might be toning up a little, you might be building some kind of man's body, but you'll always have that skinny little dick. Isn't that right?" He pulled the dildo all the way out.

Tom choked and managed to say, "Y-yes, sir."

"You'd kill to have a dick like this, wouldn't you?" Marcus hefted the machine and rubbed the head across Tom's lips, sore from the bumps and ridges on the dildo. "But if you did, you wouldn't know what to do with it, because you belong just where you are, Tommy. Bent over, greased and ready to open, like a twenty dollar whore. Isn't that right?"

"Yes sir," Tom groaned.

"Kiss it. The next time it touches you, I'll be shoving it up your ass." Marcus pointed the glistening head of the machine toward Tom's lips and he reverently kissed it. Then it was taken away. The next thing Tom felt was the awful entry of the ridged dildo. He grunted as the rings bumped their way into him. Marcus didn't leave any time to recover, but immediately started to pump the thing in and out, and Tom gripped the edges of the desk and held on.

He could scarcely believe it, but he was almost used to this by now. It was entirely unlike the day that Marcus decided to fuck him for the first time. On that day, he had had to be tied down to keep him from bolting. His jock, wet with his own fear-sweat and droplets of his own piss, was shoved in his mouth for him to bite down upon, but his anguished screams were loud enough inside his skull. That tearing pain! The dildos and the butt plugs and the copious slopping of lube had done nothing to ease that horrible, tearing pain. He cried like a child at his last violation, and endured it. By the time Marcus was finished, Tom couldn't even stand up. He was dressed and carried home and thrown into his own bed, the echoes of Frank Dobbs's laughter mocking him for days.

It took several more times before Marcus could enter without extraordinary measures, and still Tom was usually in so much discomfort that he couldn't even get stiff, let alone cum. Part of him was relieved by that, but part was also tremendously frustrated.

The pumping of the ridged dildo stopped and Marcus stood behind Tom, pressing his machine his ass. "Tell me you want it," he growled.

That too, was part of their ritual.

Tom moaned, and began the litany. "Please, Mr. Marcus, please, tear into me, fuck me, sir. I want to feel you inside me, please, I can take it, please!"

"Yes, you can take it, my little fuck-hole. Now that I've got you properly trained. Soon, you'll be able to mount it and ride it, ride my horse-cock just like a horse." Marcus leaned forward slowly and let the battering ram head of his cock begin to press into Tom's asshole.

"Tell me how you love it," came the next command.

"Oh God! Ah, ahh, ahh, I love it, sir, I love your cock, oh, God, oh, shit, please...!"

"I didn't tell you to stop." The hole opened, and Tom felt the supreme intrusion, and he gasped.

"I'm sorry, I'm sorry, please, uh! Don't stop, please fuck me, I love it, I love every inch, I want it, I want you to fuck me, fuck me, oh, God, yes!" Tom's fingers scraped along the desk, and sweat broke out all over his body. His back muscles, just starting to develop, tensed as Marcus casually slammed his cock deep into Tom's bowels.

"Yes," Marcus echoed. "Yes. That's one thing I like about you, my cocksucker, my boy-hole. You really need this. You need it with every bone in your body. You're not just saying all these things because you know that's what I want to hear. You get to a point where you really mean them."

It was true! Tom tried to shut out that hateful voice, but the truth in what the man said hurt him just as much as the vicious fucking he was getting. No, it hurt more! Because his asshole was opening up, his breath was coming in harsh gasps, and damnit, his cock was suddenly getting stiff against the woven cotton of his jock! He ground his teeth, and cursed his body even as the pain began to change, transmuting into an amazing warmth that spread through his belly and legs and into his cock.

Marcus rode the young man easily, moving his hips back and forth and watching the amazing sight of the machine at work. He always liked to do that, watch it go in that tight little hole and then come back out again. He paid no attention to Tom's gasps and moans until the sound of them changed, and then he stopped moving. Tom immediately gave a long cry of hunger.

"Oh ... my little cocksucker has decided that he really wants it today, hasn't he? You just can't stand it anymore, can you? Let's turn you over, piglet, and see what we've got." Marcus reached forward and impaled Tom on the machine in one swift thrust, and then picked the young man up.

Tom almost lost control! He was off the ground, held by Marcus' powerful arms and his monstrous cock! And Marcus was turning him!

"Get your leg up, asshole. That's it, bend it back. You don't think I'm taking my cock out of you just so you can find a new position, do you? That's it, now over! On your back!" Marcus remained utterly calm, and then dropped Tom onto his back, on the desk again. His cock was still embedded in Tom's ass. He smiled when he saw Tom's stiff cock, and reached out to grab it.

"Ha! Looks like junior wants to come out and play! OK, Tommy, you want a piece of the action? Let's see you cum first." Marcus began to jerk Tom off, his powerful, hot hand stroking Tom's cock.

"No! Oh, no, please, Mr. Marcus, please don't! I don't want to!" Tom panicked, and tried to stop Marcus, but the older man thrust violently into him and made him fall back onto the desk. His hands flew down to try to pry Marcus' off his cock.

"Don't want to come? Why not? You should, you know, it's a good use of strength, a good way to learn discipline." Marcus smiled, the efforts of fucking Tom not even beginning to show in his voice or on his face. He might have been discussing things over a cup of tea. Continuing in that casual tone, he said, "Your friend the greaser knows all about that. Yes, don't be so surprised, you think I don't know you two are holding hands and getting all lovey-dovey? I know everything you do, you little good-for-nothing asshole. Are

you in love with him? Does he make love to you?
If he does, you're not getting enough, not if you
scream and cry out for me like you're doing now.
What a joke! Two asslickers cuddling together.
Both of you put together doesn't make a whole
man."

"Please!" was all Tom could get out. The efforts
of his hands on Marcus' were not getting him anywhere, and when Marcus slapped his ass, hard,
he let his hands drop. Hearing Marcus talk about
his relationship with Will made Tom feel like he
was doubly violated. He groaned, and squirmed,
but didn't try to dislodge Marcus' hand again.

"That's better. I know why you don't want to
cum, little boy. Because your ass is going to clamp
down so hard on my dick, it'll feel like you're
passing bricks when I keep fucking you. Well,
maybe I want the feeling of your pathetic orgasm
more then I want you to be happy, did you ever
consider that, fuck-hole? The feel of your asshole
when you cum must be something like your
throat when you gag. And I don't care which one
you do, because it's my pleasure that counts, isn't
it?"

Marcus' thrusting and pumping both picked up
speed. Tom cried out in pain and pleasure, and
his back arched.

"That's right, my pleasure. So if I want to cum,
I will. And if I want to make you cum, or force you
not to, that's my decision too. Got that? I decide
here. I can give it to you or your little spic friend
anytime I want to, and I can stop it, any time I
want to! But I'm not going to stop, and you know
it. And you love it. You need it! Take it!" Slam!
Slam!

"Yes sir! Yes! Uh! Please, please, please ..." Tom didn't even know what he was asking for anymore. A shuddering wave passed through him, and he felt Marcus making his final, tortuously slow thrusts. With each punching thrust, Tom cried out, and his hands once again sought his dick, although he wasn't sure whether he needed to cum and damn the consequences, or if he was trying to stop his boss. In a second, it didn't matter. Cursing him, Marcus came, an explosion of power deep in Tom's ass, and a moment after that, Tom erupted himself, shooting cum up in the air to splatter back all over his belly.

The reflexive tightening waves of contraction that seized Tom's butthole swept along Marcus' machine, milking more manjuice from him, and he sighed in ecstasy. Tom fell back, whimpering, as Marcus plunged his dick back and forth several times to get the most pleasure from his spasming cock. Each entry seemed to hurt more, and by the time Marcus pulled out, Tom was a wreck. He let his head fall back, and brought his legs together reflexively.

"Not bad," Marcus said, stripping a well-filled scumbag off. He pulled a towel from his desk drawer and wiped himself off. "I'll have to work on the timing, though. Here." He extended his wet hand to Tom's face and Tom obediently (but weakly) began to lick it. "That's good. Good boy. You lick it up, it's good for you." And when Tom was finished to Marcus' satisfaction, he dropped the towel on the youth's stomach and told him to wipe himself off and get himself out. And somehow, Tom managed to do that.

And still, neither Tom nor Will Rodriguez could figure out how to get out of their predicament. So

Tom kept going to work every day, and showing up for training twice a week, and he endured.

Winter began to give way to spring.

CHAPTER EIGHT

VIII.

A Sunday Morning, Early Spring.

Will Rodriguez woke up slowly, coming out of a confusing dream about church and angry people, and then suddenly knowing that they really weren't angry, they just wanted to make love to him. As he began to really wake up, and he felt the warm softness around his cock, he smiled and nestled his shoulders back into the pillows. Tom was waking him up in the way Tom loved.

Under the covers, Tom licked at the bar of flesh he adored, and tasted the warm saltiness of a man after a deep sleep. He purred with pleasure. As Will's cock began to respond with a more urgent swiftness, Tom engulfed it, took it in with joy, and sucked as though it were his life's greatest pleasure. It almost was, actually.

"Ahhhh," Will sighed. "Ah, that's nice, Blondie. Shit, there's nothing like waking up this way!"

If Tom could have smiled, he would have. But he kept busy, and kept working at pleasuring, until Will called to him.

"Come on up, Blondie, come on. I want to fuck you in the shower, man. Let's get all soaped up. I've been thinking about this since yesterday!" Tom gave one last loving lick and emerged.

This was a totally new Tom. He was a far cry from the skinny college dropout who arrived in Greenwich Village almost seven months ago. He was deeply tanned, almost bronze, and his blond hair was longer than it had ever been. The current style was to wear it short, but Marcus forbade him to cut it. It was something to hold on to while he was being fucked.

And his body was fantastic. He and Will were becoming more like each other in build, tall and sculpted, but Tom was starting to build some power in his back and arms that Will just didn't have. Together, with their deep chests, their firm, washboard stomachs and their broad shoulders, they often got wolf whistles on the street.

Tom followed Will obediently into the bathroom, and started the water running. They got in together and kissed, and began to soap each other up, laughing and tickling, and then getting firmer and more passionate. Soon, they were locked together, the warm water cascading over them both, their cocks pressed together. They stayed that way for a while, and then Will turned away to reach for the basket of rubbers. Laughing, he chose one with ribs, and Tom sank down to his knees to put it on, using his mouth to smooth it over the flesh.

More soap and more fondling followed, and then Tom opened himself for his lover. Locked together once again, they rocked and pumped under the falling water, their groans muted and their pleasure great. Will came with several swift, powerful thrusts; Tom cried out with him. Tenderly, they rinsed each other off and dried themselves, and Will got back in bed.

"That was nice," Tom said, heading into the kitchen. "I love any day that starts like that."

"Yeah," Will agreed. "You are one fine cocksucker, Blondie. I keep telling you, there's money to be made there."

"Sorry. One *puta* in the family's enough!"

"Your mother!"

Tom laughed as he put the coffee on. Will had often regretted enriching Tom's vocabulary. He poured two cups and put the rest back on the plate to keep it warm, and came back to the bed. He passed one cup to his glowering lover, who relaxed a little and smirked.

"You got a mouth on you, Blondie, and this time, I don't mean cocksucking!" He took the cup and sipped. "So, how're you feeling? Any better?"

"Fine." Tom had come over late on Friday night, exhausted, dirty, and sore all over. As usual, Will hadn't asked any questions. This was the first time he made any reference to it.

"That's cool."

They didn't live together. Will needed his own space on most weeknights, and Tom was thankful that he still had his own refuge. No matter how good he felt when he was with his lover, there were times when he just needed to be alone. But almost every weekend, they ended up at one apartment or the other.

There were exceptions of course. Will's customers didn't turn off their needs on weekends, and sometimes he would call Tom during the week and tell him he was going to be away for a few days. Tom would feed his cats and sleep in his bed anyway, smelling him in the sheets and dreaming of him. And that was something else they didn't talk about. Sometimes they seemed to be living a life of secrets.

This morning, the secrets weighed heavily on Tom's mind, and he immediately regretted answering Will's question so quickly. He drank more coffee and leaned back against the wall, composing his thoughts.

"Will, I'm not really fine," he said finally.

"Huh? What do you mean? You don't feel good? You got no bruises."

"No, no. My body is fine. But … I'm not well in a different way. I'm sick of living like this. I'm depressed and afraid all the time. It's like you're the only good thing in my life." The words spilled out artlessly, but Tom was glad they did.

Will put his mug down and shifted in bed. "Well, shit, I know that, Tom. What do you think, I forgot? What do you want to do, see a shrink or something?"

"No!" Tom laughed at the idea. "You know what a shrink would say. If I came out to my parents and pressed charges, everything would come out in the open, people would respect me for it, and my depression would stop." His shoulders shook with ironic mirth.

"Hey, you don't know that, man. I mean,

shrinks see criminals all the time, and I bet they aren't telling them to go turn themselves in, you know? If you don't want to, that's OK. But if you're not gonna do those things, and you're not gonna go dump on some guy to listen to you and give you happy pills, then what do you want to do? Really? What use is it talking about it; it's not going away. It's not changing, man." Will didn't mean to sound harsh, and Tom knew that he was only trying to keep things in perspective.

"Well, it's not going to change if we never change it," Tom said. "I think we better start trying of thinking of ways to change it."

"You're out of your mind, Blondie. What are you gonna do, change Marcus? Convince him it's not nice to do what he does? Shit, he's more uptight then ever these days."

"Oh? Why?"

Will's dark eyes took on the glint that appeared whenever he was about to share a juicy secret. "He's got this friend, out in California? Started out sucking his cock, like everybody else, but check it out, this guy owns some gyms out there now. He's turned out to be some big-time body-builder himself, he's on the covers of a few magazines in the office. Marcus talks to him all the time, they're buddies, kinda."

"Yeah? So?" Tom couldn't make any connection.

"Well, this guy and Marcus, they have a cute scam going. They trade students, see? He sends some to New York, and Marcus sends some to California. But they only trade their special students, you know, the ones with a video library attached."

Tom felt slightly ill. He imagined being shipped

173

off like so much freight, to fall into a similar life with a complete stranger.

"Yeah, it's a pretty lousy deal for the kids, but these guys don't care. This way, they get to rotate the stock. Pretty boy out in LA gets some stocky Italian guys and a black guy every once in a while, and Marcus gets some golden California boy."

"So ..?"

"I'm getting to it, Blondie, shit, you know how to ruin a good story! The point here, is that they haven't made a trade in months. 'Cause Marcus isn't holding up his end of the deal, OK? If you haven't noticed, business is down. And his last new boy, kiddo, was your blond ass. And he should have sent you out, as, you know, courtesy, but he didn't."

Tom sighed. "Jesus, I don't know what to feel about that. I'm glad I wasn't traded, but if I had to live like this, it might have been nicer to live in California. But what about ... I mean, if he had to, why didn't he ... You're pretty hot...."

Will grinned. "Two reasons, Blondie. One, he still thinks of me as his special project, and we don't have to talk about that, OK? Two, the guy in LA, he's a fucking bigot. He don't want no greasers, and that's the way he fucking says it, too. But what does he know? All they got out there is Mexicans, man, they don't know from one Hispanic to another. Same problem Marcus has, 'cause he spent so much time out there."

"You mean his problem is that he doesn't know which curse is right for you?"

"Yeah! I mean, it's almost as bad as being called a Cuban, man. Or a Dominican." Will shivered in mock horror.

"So, let me get this straight. Marcus is upset because he isn't trading with this guy? Why?"

"Because it makes him look bad, kiddo. And nothing is worse to a bodybuilder then looking bad, OK? And because he isn't getting new toys to play with, and his old ones aren't in competition form, and they're not so happy anymore, and business is bad. It's a lot of stuff all together, man. So I don't think he'll be listening to reason, you know?" Will finished his coffee with a few gulps and handed the mug to Tom. "Go get me another cup, OK? I don't want to get up yet."

Tom went off to the kitchen and refilled both mugs. Then he rinsed out the coffeepot and refilled it with water and scoops of fresh coffee and thought about what Will had just told him. There was something there, something good, but what could they do about it? He poured milk into the coffee and returned to the bed as the coffee machine began to make more. Will was stretching, and Tom stopped to admire him as he did.

"Well, don't just stand there, Blondie! Shit, you'd think you never seen me naked before." But Will grinned all the same.

"Will, I think I'm starting to have an idea," Tom said, getting into the bed. "No, really. Do you think there's some way we can use these things against Marcus? Do you think some of the other guys at the gym might help?"

"Help do what? They're as afraid as you are. What could they do, threaten to strike?" He grinned. "I don't think it's gonna work, little brother. As long as he has those tapes, he's in control."

"Yeah, maybe. But if we ganged up, if we

175

worked together, maybe we could figure out a way
to get those tapes and destroy them. Maybe ..."

"Maybe we can grow wings and fly, too!"

"No, Will, I mean it! Take me seriously, OK?"
Tom's voice hardened, and when Will really
looked at him, he grew more serious.

"OK, Blondie, OK, I was only kidding you.
What do you want to do?"

"I don't know!" Tom cried out in frustration.
"But there must be a way to use his own 'boys'
against him. To use all the hatred he builds up in
people and turn it back on him."

"Well, I like that," Will admitted. "Let's give it
some more thought. In the mean time, I could
sure use some more of your mouth, Blondie. Lay
down, that's it, put that shit down. I want you to
suck on this like you did this morning ... yeah,
like that."

Whatever annoyance Tom had about being
interrupted in mid-plan vanished as he slid down
onto his side, his head toward Will's feet, and
sucked Will's cock into his mouth. By now, he
knew exactly what Will liked, and he lavished
attention on the head and the membrane of flesh
over it that he loved so much.

"Yeah, you know it, Blondie, you know it, get
your tongue deep in there, yeah, like that...." Will
cupped Tom's ass in his hand and pulled the
young man closer to his body. Slowly, he began to
slide down the bed, and Tom reacted by taking his
cock deeper into his mouth and wrapping one arm
around his leg.

"Oh, that's nice, Blondie, hold on tight, daddy's
gonna take you for a nice ride today!"

Will's hand closed gently around Tom's cock

and balls, drawing them together like a cockring, and he tugged. Tom moaned around the tool in his mouth, appreciating the feeling, and Will kept on teasing him. Rolling together on the bed, they maneuvered into the position Will wanted, as he slid one arm around one of Tom's legs.

Tom kept happily sucking and licking and playing with Will's cock, anticipating Will either spilling his cum all over his chest, or driving up his ass again, and he almost didn't realize what was happening when he felt warmth cover his own cock.

Will had curled his body so that his mouth was right over Tom's cock, and he very slowly took it in. It took Tom a few seconds to react, he was so surprised.

Will had never sucked his cock before.

Not that Tom felt that this was lacking in his life! He was perfectly happy to jerk off, or to be jerked off, and much more happy when Will fucked him in either hole. But it never occurred to him to ask for this favor.

He moaned and his entire body tensed. He tried to pull away, and it was in his mind to protest, 'You don't have to do that!', but Will pulled away first.

"Stop sucking my cock, Blondie, and I'll fucking bite yours off, OK? If you're mine, everything belongs to me, and if I wanna do this, I get to, so just put that mouth back where it belongs and mind your own fucking business!"

Tom gladly put his mouth back where it belonged and sucked with all the energy and talent he could muster. Will played with the pale dick before him, licking it and nibbling on it, flip-

177

ping it back and forth in his fingers, jacking it off a little and then taking it all the way into his throat, and then going back to licking.

Tom moaned and groaned and grasped Will's leg like a life preserver. The pleasure that was shooting through his body was almost unbearable! But he knew how to contain his own orgasm, and he held on, using all of his strength and trying to focus on giving Will pleasure.

It was Tom who broke first, though. Pulling his head back, he gasped out, "Oh, God, you gotta stop! I'm gonna cum any minute!"

Will pulled back immediately and asked, "You want it on you or in you?"

"On me! I wanna feel it!"

"On your fucking back!"

Tom threw himself on his back, his cock painfully erect and glistening, and his hand flew down to grasp it. Will straddled his legs, and began jerking off as well, and arched his back as cum jetted out of his dick onto Tom's tight belly. Tom felt like he was roaring when his own cum started to shoot, and it mingled with Will's to pool and drip across his stomach. The two men gasped and took deep breaths, and Will rolled over onto his back.

"Still the same Blondie," he said finally.

"Huh?"

"You still like to make a mess on the bed. You wanted it, you clean it up."

Tom was too happy to be annoyed. He cleaned, and when he came back and saw that Will was starting to get dressed, he had a broad smile on his face.

"What's with you, other then the fact that you got what you wanted?"

"Will … I think I have an idea. I think we can do it, too. But I'll need your help."

The darker man looked up suspiciously. "You know, this isn't playing games here. If we fuck up, Marcus is gonna make our lives fucking miserable. More miserable then they are, OK?"

"Yeah, I know. But what are we if we don't try?"

Will shrugged. "OK, you convinced me. Tell me about your plan."

Tom sat down and did. By the end of the afternoon, they were making calls. By that evening; they were too hopeful to even talk about it.

By Tuesday night of that week, while Tom was being worked to exhaustion, he knew that the plan had already started.

CHAPTER NINE

IX.

As spring gathered its momentum, a subtle change began to occur at the Gold Medal Gym. It was so subtle that no one noticed it for days, and even then, they doubted that it was a genuine change. It was just that some of the men were getting more moody then usual.

Part of it was an increase in silence. Discussions would falter or just stop when Frank Dobbs entered a room. Alex, usually quite a talker, began to whistle more and talk less. Jimmy, one of Marcus' "special" trainees, missed a session and suffered silently for it, an expression of stoicism that was unlike him. Rodriguez, who rarely came to the gym for anything more then his required workouts and private sessions, began to appear during the day. He was often found in the lounge, or in the pool rooms. And far too often, he was found with one of the managers or staff members.

The customers remained the same, more or less. Actually, less. There were fewer new memberships in the gym that season than there ever were. Some blamed it on the economy, some on the explosion of new neighborhood gyms with pastel walls and stylish logos and designer workout clothes in the window. Some blamed it on the fact that it was a men's gym. Gyms with an open admissions policy got more members, they argued. A lot of folks went to gyms to find lovers.

Marcus never commented on that, except to say that if the only reason you were going to a gym was to get laid, he didn't want you at his gym. His staff used to laugh when he said that, their laughter the honest affirmation of men supporting a manly pursuit. Lately, though, their laughs were tinged with sarcasm and irony.

Marcus didn't like that.

Neither did he like the fact that several long-time gym members turned in their locker keys and cards and told him that they had found other gyms to go to. He pressed them politely: what could he do to keep them there? Their answers were frustratingly dissimilar. Enlarge the place, said one man, who was joining a club that had indoor tennis and racquetball. I'm moving uptown, said another. I need a less impact-oriented program, said another.

Marcus enjoyed teaching one or two of his boys proper respect when he felt that they were acting too sullen or resentful, but after those enjoyable sessions, he retreated to his office to ponder what had really happened. Why on earth would any of them suddenly develop a resentful attitude with him? How dare they even think of defying him, even dream that he would be satisfied with their half-hearted obedience? Despite the lack of any real evidence, he began to believe that the sudden drop in customers and the rise in insolence from his property had to be connected.

He began to wander around the club more, trying to catch anyone doing or saying anything that supported his theory. But much to his frustration, the day-to-day operation of the gym went smoothly, people showed up on time and did their tasks, and they continued to come when he called them and submit to his demands.

He turned to his second in command one evening, after a particularly satisfying session with Rodriguez. They were both at Marcus' home, an elegantly masculine retreat uptown, far away from the noise and dirt of the lower east side.

He had kicked the brown bastard out after the two of them had their fill of him, and Frank was about to leave when Marcus asked, suddenly, "What's happening at the gym?"

"Huh? What do you mean, boss?"

"I mean, what's happening there? I had to slap Johnny around the other night, he didn't seem like he was too happy about sucking my cock. And what's with the Puerto Rican, too? He was awful quiet tonight. What the hell is going on?"

Dobbs thought about it, a process which did not lend any more intelligence to his ugly face. Finally, he shrugged. "I dunno, boss. Things seem OK to me. Business is a little slow, but it'll pick up."

Marcus stared at him for a moment, and seemed about to say something else, but instead, he waved one hand. "Never mind. Get out, I'll see you tomorrow. You have a session with Tom tomorrow night, right?"

"Yep."

"We'll do it together. Maybe the little bastard is talking to the other guys. If so, we can get it out of him. If not, he needs a refresher course anyway; he's getting too cocky."

"Yeah, a little. How come you didn't send him to LA, boss? He woulda been good out there. You haven't had fresh meat in a while, y'know?"

Marcus stood up, his anger controlled. Stark naked, the power emanated from his body, and Frank Dobbs, who was afraid of no man, took a step back.

"I didn't ask for your input or your opinion, Frank. If I wanted to send him, I would. Now get your ass out of here, before I try some old meat on for size."

Frank Dobbs left. Immediately.

"He's involved," Marcus said to himself as he made himself a drink. "That little fucking blond bastard has to be involved. Well, he's going to regret it. By the time I'm finished with him, he won't be of any use to anyone." He balled one fist up, and stroked it. "Especially that little cocksucking spic."

Tom's day went by as usual. It dragged a little yet ended early, as all days that ended with a private session did. What made things worse was the rumor passed to him by a note shoved in his locker, that Marcus and Dobbs were going to see him

186

tonight. It was usually one or the other, Frank more than Marcus. If they were both going to see him, he was in for an evening of hell. At lunchtime, he called Rodriguez and passed the word on.

Tom reported to the private workout room in shorts and a tank top, but removed both at once. A clean jock was his only allowed garment for sessions. He got there first, so he mutely set the equipment up and waited, and tried to act surprised when Marcus and Dobbs walked in.

"OK, you soft, sorry sonofabitch, get down and give me a hundred," Dobbs said as he tossed his equipment bag down, "the boss wants to see what you can do these days." Marcus sat on the bench to watch, and the session began.

If Tom was worried that the session might be more brutal then usual, he was correct. But worse, it was far more humiliating then usual. After the initial steps, designed to get him warmed up and ready for the real work, almost every new exercise violated him, pinched him, exposed him, or made him wince and turn red with shame. Those awful clamps, now bearing huge weights, came out of the bag and locked onto his nipples when he was on his back again, and every pump of his arms brought them tighter and looser on his tender nipples. But at the same time, Dobbs worked that ridged dildo in and out of his asshole while his legs were tied straight up and back. His back ached, his asshole burned and his tits fairly screamed on their own. And while this was happening, Marcus merely sat and watched.

They made him fuck himself on a buttplug planted on one of the low benches and held in

place by Frank's foot. He did a series of deep
squats over it, the weights now attached to his
balls, one weight on either side of the bench.
Every time he went down, the pressure on his
balls lessened and his ass was stretched open.
Every time he went up, his balls tightened and
his ass closed. Exhaustion was not an option. He
whimpered when they pulled him up and tugged
the clips off. It was the first real sound he had
made that night, other then the grunts of muscular effort.

Marcus really didn't like that.

"You must think you're getting tough," the boss
said, as Tom drank gratefully from the water bottle Frank passed him. "You have no idea how
wrong you are, cocksucker. Get over here and get
this in your fucking useless mouth."

Tom obediently crawled over to the man and
opened his jaws to take the head of the machine.
Marcus, worried or not, was as huge as ever. He
crammed more of it suddenly into Tom's mouth
and held him firmly in place.

"I don't know what you think you're doing, you
and your little Spanish loverboy, but it's going to
stop tonight. You're going to see exactly what you
are around here, boy, and it's not going to be a
pretty sight. Before I'm finished with you tonight,
about the only thing you're going to be good for is
what you're doing now, choking on my fat cock."
He pulled him back suddenly, and Tom gasped a
quick breath in before he was re-impaled.

Using his hair as a leash, Marcus continued
doing this for a while, holding Tom in place long
enough for Tom to start to struggle for air, letting
him take a breath, and then plugging him up

again. Before long, involuntary tears formed in Tom's eyes, and Marcus sighed. This was more like what he wanted!

He stopped and stood up. "Come on, Frank, you take his mouth, I'm going for a dip in his butthole."

"Sure you don't want me to open it up a little more, boss?"

"Oh, I'm sure he's wide open, Frank...."

The two men moved Tom for their comfort, and Tom ended up bent over the bench, his legs straight and his elbows leaning against the padding. Dobbs bared his cock and neatly speared Tom's throat and sighed.

Marcus spread Tom's asscheeks and began to press inward.

"Oh, yes, that's open enough," he said, as he plowed forward. "But not nearly as open as he's going to be before the night is out. Isn't that right, Frank?"

"Sure is, boss, sure is! Wanna tell him what's up?"

"Later, Frank, later. Let him wonder. And let's get some pleasure out of him before we limit his usefulness."

That said, the two men fell to seriously raping their captive. And Tom was caught in the middle, a cock on both ends, the one in his mouth covered with a rank foreskin, to be sure, but a hated cock nonetheless. He choked on the crooked dick, its knotted surface such a huge change from the silken ball and horn that was Marcus' machine and the smooth beauty of Will's. He closed his eyes and tried to relax, tried to take the double impalement. The pounding and stretching of his rear seemed almost bearable, as long as he could hold on and stay calm ... he had to stay calm....

Marcus slapped his ass several times before the big man came, and Tom was almost grateful for the fleshy gag that kept him from crying out. Marcus was a brutal fucker when he came, slamming his cock forcefully into whatever aperture was available, all the way to the root. When he pulled out, the blond youth sighed and shivered, but kept sucking.

He had been trained well.

"You keep him entertained, Frank. I'm going to get the rest of our cast for tonight."

As the door closed behind him, Frank pulled his cock out of Tom's mouth and gave the youth a condom to unwrap. "Get it on me, fucker, quick. I'm gonna use that ass of yours before the boss ruins it!"

Tom quickly did as Frank told him and shook as Frank took up his position. What had the ugly man meant? What was going to happen to him? Did he mean to suggest that Marcus' cock was going to do the ruining, or was this something that had to do with what Marcus had been talking about?

Frank shoved in the passage so recently vacated by his boss and shuddered in pleasure. With no finesse or care for Tom's comfort, he immediately began his high-speed, high-force fucking, designed to get his rocks off as soon as possible. He was out and clean by the time Marcus returned.

Marcus wasn't alone. In fact, he really did bring a group back with him.

Alex and John were there, Alex carrying his gear bag and wearing his jacket, as though he was just leaving. Larry was there, and Jimmy as well. But must surprisingly, so was Rodriguez. They crowded into the small room, and Marcus, holding onto Rodriguez by one arm, spoke.

"We're all here tonight to witness something and to learn a lesson. Tommy here has been acting bad lately. So has his little pussy boy, Willie. But I'm not so angry at Willie, because he's a mutt, a cheap sucking hustler who'd blow dogs if he was hard up for cash. And you can't blame an animal for doing something that's in its nature.

"But Tommy here, he should have known better. I'm partly to blame here, because I let him hang out with this piece of cheap trash, and maybe I gave him more freedom then he should have had. But let me tell you one thing, right now. *I am still in charge*. I am still in control here. I made a good life for you bastards, and I don't like to be thanked with whispers and plots. So I hope that watching what's going to happen and being a part of it will help remind you all who's the master here."

He pushed Rodriguez into the middle of the room and told him to strip down. He did, and as Frank dragged Tom out of the way, Tom couldn't help but feel that incredible lust for his lover that he always felt when he was taking his clothing off. He tensed in Frank's arms, and Frank only gripped him tighter.

Will was turned around and bent over the same bench that Will had been on. Marcus handcuffed him to one of the lower crossbars so that he couldn't rise, and then nodded at Frank. Frank pushed Tom over to Marcus, and took up his leather belt.

191

"No, please, Mr. Marcus, let me take it, please, he didn't do anything!" Tom shouted, struggling against Marcus' grip.

"Oh? And did you do something, cocksucker?" Marcus pulled him closer and with one hand pulled his jockstrap down. He gripped the youth's cock and began to manipulate it. "If you tell me, we'll let him go right now."

"No! No, I didn't do anything, we didn't, please, Mr. Marcus, please don't … ahhh!"

Marcus squeezed his balls casually, and shook him. "Then you'd better shut your mouth, boy. Or better yet, go and get your favorite gag!" He pushed Tom down on his knees and slammed his cock into Tom's mouth again.

The rest all watched in silence as Frank savagely beat Will, on his ass and legs and across his shoulders. Will took it all, gritting his teeth and making growling noises, but not more then that. The heat in the room became oppressive. When Frank finished, everyone was sweating, and Tom was whimpering around his "gag."

"Now, this is what's going to happen," Marcus said, holding Tom by the hair. "This little cocksucker is going to learn how to fuck. He's going to get his pathetic little dick into the asshole of his boyfriend over there. It should be nice and comfortable now that Frank's warmed it up a little. And to encourage him to have good fucking habits, the rest of you guys are all going to take turns in his ass. We'll drop the little bags of cum right on his boyfriend's back so he can keep count. And if anyone wants seconds, they're encouraged to take them. Because after you're all finished, I'm gonna take my hand and I'm going to open him up real big. And when my fist is in there, I'll open it up and shove my cock in and jerk off in his asshole. After that, he'll be sitting on fireplugs to fill that butthole."

Tom shook and began to struggle, and managed to pull his head away. "No! No, please ..."

"I didn't ask you, asshole." Marcus easily pushed Tom to the ground and ripped his jockstrap off. As Tom howled his protests and fears, Marcus stuffed the jock into his mouth and picked him up.

"Hey, Mr. Marcus, can I use the spic's mouth while we're getting warmed up?" asked Alex.

"Sure, I don't see why not. But save your cum for this one's ass."

"I wouldn't miss it, boss!"

Marcus felt much better. His boys were back, if they had ever really left at all. They would never forget this night, not the pleasure he offered them or the punishment he delivered. He tossed Tom into the arms of Larry and John and said, "Tie his hands behind his back; he doesn't need them for fucking. And get him hard enough to fuck. Jimmy, you come over here and suck my cock while we watch. We'll let Larry and John go first, then you, and then Alex."

Marcus bent over to strip off his sweatpants, and hardly knew what hit him.

It was Jimmy, the man who Frank Dobbs had so brutally used one morning in the private shower room while an innocent Tom Kake watched. He had started to nod at Marcus' order, but as soon as Marcus bent over, he launched himself at the man's legs. Entangled in the soft cotton pants, Marcus went down, hard. In an instant, Alex leapt for his head, and slammed it against the floor.

Dobbs, who was stroking his crooked cock back up to a fucking state, stood amazed. The boys attacking Mr. Marcus just did not register in his mind. By the time he woke up and started to move, Larry and John, who had dropped their hold on Tom, jumped him and bore him backward, against the wall. He roared like a bull and shook John off easily, but Larry held on tenaciously, just long enough for Tom, with his jockstrap still half in his mouth, to make a vicious kick and land it directly on that already crooked cock.

Dobbs howled! He bent forward, and John connected with a clean upward shot to the jaw, sending the ugly man back into the wall again.

By the time things were quiet again, there was a clear victory. Jimmy, Alex and Will, handcuffs still dangling from one wrist, were sitting on Marcus. They struggled with the big man and got him on his belly, and picked up the key from the floor near the bench.

"Good thing this was in your hand when you came over for your blow job, man," Will said to Alex as he unlocked the other cuff.

"Good thing all handcuff keys are alike," agreed Alex, who was busy trying to hold one of Marcus' arms down. They did, and finally the cuffs were on him. The other pair went on a much-dazed Frank Dobbs.

"You assholes are going to regret this!" Marcus screamed, pulling against the cuffs. "I'll get out of these, and you're all dead meat! You're going to have to let us go eventually! If you do it now, I swear, I'll let you live, but if you keep me like this for one more minute, you are dead! Do you understand me? Dead!"

"I think he talks too much," Will said. Tom tossed him the jockstrap, and they forced it into his mouth, binding it in place with an ace bandage.

"Well?" Alex asked, as they leaned back and surveyed their captives. "Now what?"

"Now," Tom said, putting his shorts back on, "we get the video camera."

CHAPTER TEN

X.

Using Marcus' keys, Tom and Alex got into the inner office and began to ransack it. They found a cabinet on one wall where the camera was stored. There was a pile of blank tapes next to it, and they took them, but they didn't stop there. They kept checking all the drawers and shelves for where Marcus kept his blackmail tapes.

"Damn! They're not here!" Alex swore.

"No, they're here," Tom said, looking around. "Any guy with a hidden camera knows how to hide other things, too. Let's go back and see if we can persuade one of them to tell us where they are."

"You know, you're not bad, Tom," Alex said. "I'm sorry about, you know ..."

199

"Yeah, well, I don't wanna think about that now."

They went back to the room. John and Larry left to empty out the gym and close it down for the night. While Tom and Alex were gone, though, the other three men had gotten a little more creative with their captives.

Frank Dobbs was practically up on his toes. His hands were locked behind his back, but coils of rope were wrapped around his chest and drawn back behind him and tied to the top bar on the equipment rack. He was naked, and a bootlace was wrapped around his cock and balls, making them even more ugly then they naturally were. His mouth was stuffed with someone's jockstrap, and his ankles were strapped together with another ace bandage.

Marcus was on his belly on the bench. His head was tied down with the bandage that had been around his mouth, and his legs were spread wide and tied down at the thighs, knees, and ankles. The ropes dug into his muscles and left red and white lines as he struggled. When the two men with the camera came back, Will was using Frank's belt on Marcus' ass and legs, cursing fluently in Spanish and moving his arm with demonic fury.

Tom picked up the camera and turned it on. "Let's start this movie, shall we?" he said, moving in.

The camera swept the helpless body of the owner of the Gold Medal Gym, his contorted, bright red face, his straining back muscles, his bound legs, and, when Will stopped long enough, Alex spread the man's ass cheeks for a close-up.

"How do you like being a star?" Tom asked, focusing the camera for a better view.

"You are dead," the man growled out of the corner of his mouth. "Do you hear me? Dead!"

"Not before you suffer," Will interjected. He slashed the belt down across Marcus' thighs and then his calves, and started working savagely on the man's legs. "This is for every time you did this to me, you motherfucker!"

"I'm gonna get all of you!" Marcus screamed, fighting his bonds.

Tom passed the camera to Alex and picked up a toy dropped before, the ridged dildo. "I think we have to do something to keep that mouth busy," he said, moving to the front of the bench. Marcus tried to keep his teeth clenched, but Tom merely pinched his nose, and when he opened his mouth to breathe, thrust the dildo as far in as it would go.

Marcus gagged, and his entire body jerked against the bonds.

"He's not very good at sucking cock," Tom noted, pulling the dildo out a little and then shoving it back in.

"We will have to give him some practice," Will responded, hitting even harder.

When John and Larry came back, they got serious. Each man took up the strap and used it on the bound man, until his entire back, from shoulders to calves, was red and bruised. Tom used the dildo with a savage arm, fucking Marcus' mouth as though the fuckstick was his own dick. He watched the man's lips getting bruised, and watched the convulsions of his throat and chest and stomach every time he gagged, and he thought, 'There! That's what it feels like! Take it! For every time you did this to me!'

Everyone seemed to have that same idea. Then Tom pulled the dildo out of Marcus's mouth and demanded, "Where are the video tapes?"

"Go to hell!" was his only reply.

"OK. We'll find out sooner or later. If not from you, then from him." Tom looked over at Frank Dobbs and wiped the dildo off in Marcus' hair. "He looks lonely, guys. Anyone want to keep him company?"

"Yeah, I owe him some of these," John said, panting. He was the last one to take the belt to Marcus. "And a few more things, too."

"Good. You start on him, and we'll turn this cutie over. I have a few things I really want him to feel. I need some help here."

John and Jimmy went over to Frank Dobbs with two belts and wicked gleams in their eyes. Before long, their timed blows echoed through the room. One at a time they swung, smacking thighs and chest, catching nipples and belly, arms and legs, and the more Frank tried to protect himself, the harder they hit. Soon he was turning under their blows, so they could get his ass and shoulders too.

The other men teamed up to turn Marcus over. Before they did that, though, they greased up one of those huge butt plugs that was in Frank Dobb's bag and shoved it forcefully up his ass, his curses ringing against the walls.

"He is too tight!" Will laughed. "We're gonna have to loosen him up!"

"Don't worry, we will," promised Tom. They then performed the maneuver to turn him over. It wasn't easy; he fought them every inch of the way. But they were strong, too, and they were trained by him. They did it, and tied him back down, with his head over one end of the bench and his thighs spread wide.

"Wait," Will said, studying the prone man. "I got something special I wanna do. Wait for me." He left in a hurry.

When he came back, he had a wet towel, a cup, and a disposable razor. The other men grinned as Will wet down Marcus' pubic area and began to shave his hair off.

"You sonofabitch, when I get free, you're gonna be first, do you hear me!"

"Hey, man, you better hold still. If I slip too much, it could be nasty." Will kept on shaving, and when he wiped the area clean, they shoved the towel into Marcus' mouth. Alex brought the camera in for another close up. Without the nest of curls, the monstrous cock seemed even more monsterlike, rising from red and white skin.

"OK, that's the master. How's the dog?"

Frank Dobbs was striped an angry red all over his body. His bound-up cock and balls had gotten several shots, and he sagged against the ropes in agony. Will went over to him and pulled the gag out of his mouth. "How about you tell us where the tapes are, cutie? Before we get down to seriously hurting you!"

"You motherfucking, sonof-mmmm! Mmph!" Will crammed the gag back in. "OK, I got that. Turn him around, guys, Marcus wet down this present for him, I better give it up." They did as he asked, and he produced the ridged dildo. "Oh," he said in mock surprise. "Look, it's not as wet as

I thought. Well, what can you do, right, man? In it goes!"

With one mighty thrust, the fuckstick was pushed past the tight opening to Frank's asshole and buried deep within! His body shot up until he was standing full on his toes, and the muffled scream that they heard behind the gag brought smiles to some of their faces.

"That felt good," Will said, letting the handle go. The dildo stayed, wedged in. "Almost as good as it's gonna feel when I fuck him."

Sounds of restrained movement and a muffled series of curses drew his attention over to the bench, where Tom was busy picking up and dropping weights attached to Marcus' nipples by those toothed clamps. He had run the cord up and over a bar, and was dropping the weights from different heights to see what reaction he got.

"I've waited so long to see him like this," Tom said, lifting the weights over his head. "Now you're starting to know what it feels like, you bastard." He dropped them, and the teeth dug into the man's nipples, and his chest rose under the bonds.

They took Dobbs down from his bondage and using the dildo up his ass as a handle, propelled him to the bench, where he was bent over, his face in Marcus' crotch. They pulled his gag out. "Get to work, fuckface!" Jimmy growled. "Get your mouth over it and start getting it down!"

While Jimmy held Frank's nose shut, Will tied a workout boot to the cords binding Frank's cock and balls. It swung back and forth, tightening the cords and pulling at the meat.

When Frank was compelled to open his mouth

and forced down onto the machine, they looped an ace bandage around his neck and under the bench, and the men started to line up to either beat his ass or work the dildo in and out. Tom continued to torture Marcus' tits.

"OK, get outa my way! I wanna be first to plow that bastard!" Will bared his cock and slid a rubber on with practiced ease. He jerked the dildo out and tossed it away and shoved his own cock in with a long sigh. The men cheered, and Frank's muffled reaction was lost, barely felt by the man whose cock was stretching his mouth open. A puddle of drool and spit was forming in Marcus' crotch. With every thrust forward, the workout boot swayed and tugged.

"What a sight," John said, taking his own cock in his hand. "I can't fucking stand it. This is too good!"

"Not yet," muttered Tom. "It's not enough yet!"

Will came madly, slapping Frank's ass when he did, and crying out, "Take it, you fucking *maricon!* Take it all!" When he pulled out, he tied his scumbag up and tossed it onto Marcus' belly, just in front of Frank's face. "I'm saving my next load for you, Marcus!"

"I'm next!"

"No, me!"

The men jostled for position, but it was John who followed Will. And Jimmy who followed John.

They took a break, looking at the three globes of cum lying on Marcus' stomach, the wasted look in Frank's eyes, and the ravaged nipples, torn by those toothed clamps. Tom reached forward and quickly took them off, and Marcus roared behind his gag.

"It's a good start," Tom said, snapping the clamps open and closed. "But the big guy here needs some plowing of his own."

"Yeah!"

"Get Frank off there!"

"What are we gonna do with him?"

They pulled Frank up, and spit ran from his mouth. He coughed and they were shocked to see tears on his face. "Let me go," were the first words out of his mouth. "My God, let me go, I'll never say a fucking word, I swear!"

"Well, I'll be fucked!" Alex said.

"Tell us where the tapes are," Tom interjected.

"Lower right drawer in the desk! There's a button on the inside, left side! It opens the closet. I swear! Go look! Just let me go!"

Tom pointed at Jimmy and Alex. "Go look." They did, and when they came back, they had armloads of tapes, all labeled with men's names and dates. The men rushed to look at them, and whistles and muttered curses followed.

"There's about, what, nearly a hundred guys here!"

"Look, he's got three tapes of you, Will."

"He's even got two tapes of Frank!"

They looked at the broken man and he lowered his head.

"What a fucking wimp," Will said, amazed. "Shit, and he was calling *me* weak? I'm gonna fuckin' kill him!"

"Wait," Tom said, looking at the four tapes with his name on them. "We're not finished with him yet, even though he told us where the tapes were. I have a way of taking care of this."

Under his direction, they picked Frank Dobbs

up, untied the boot from his nuts, and made him straddle Marcus' face. Then, pulling out the gag, they compelled Marcus to take Dobbs' ugly dick into his mouth.

"Now, you're in his hands, Frank ... or at least, his mouth. If he bites down, that's between you and him. Let's see if he's as loyal to you as you were to him!" Tom then directed a small change in bondage, and they lifted Marcus' legs up and tied them back, exposing his asshole, with the fat plug still buried inside.

"Now, we get some revenge," Tom said, taking his shorts off.

They all fucked him. All five of them took turns in Marcus' ass, and all the while he had Frank's cock in his mouth. The pile of used condoms grew bigger. When they each had him once, the belt came back, and when they were tired of that, their cocks took over again.

It was a brutal, sweaty attack. Little more was said, their hatred was so deep. Instead, they concentrated on hurting him, punishing him. Finally, Tom stood over the scene, and they pulled Frank away so Marcus could see them. They were on to their second video tape. Tom held the tapes up.

"This is how it's going to be, Marcus," he said. "We have these tapes. We also have our own tapes back. If you ever make trouble for any one of us again, these tapes go out. Now, we may not be able to find your mom and dad, and they may not care, but I can think of a lot of sleazy papers and cable shows that would love to get their hands on tapes like these."

"You ... you little bastard." Even through all that abuse, Marcus was undefeated. He strained against the ropes once for effect. "I'm going to get your ass one of these days!"

"I don't think so, Mr. Marcus. *Ronnie.*"

Tom pulled a condom onto his cock. It was as hard as it had ever been, and the constriction sent a rush through him as he stepped forward. Easily, he slid into Marcus' well-used hole, the first time he fucked that night. Marcus ground his teeth and tried to shift his massive frame away, but the bonds held. The men cheered Tom on, and heaped verbal abuse onto the man who had held them all in sexual slavery for so long.

Tom hadn't fucked anyone in ages ... not since Scott. Despite its stretching, Marcus' butthole was unused to this treatment, and it felt warm and tight. Tom sighed and smiled, much to the amusement of his co-conspiritors. He caught Will's grin, and began to move faster, spilling his seed in an angry rush. When he pulled out, instead of tying his condom up and tossing it into the growing pile, he upended it and spilled the contents on the bloated, ignored machine.

The men laughed and worked one last time to change their captives' positions. The two men ended up on the floor, their hands still handcuffed behind their backs. They were cock-to-mouth, and bandages wrapped around their shoulders, necks and heads held them that way. Additional ropes wrapped them around their waists and ankles.

Two handcuff keys were produced, and it was Alex who decided where to put them. Dropping each one in a condom, he then shoved them, one in each man's ass, tucking them in deep. "You can get your heads free and suck 'em out, if you want, or wait until something else pushes them out!"

The little scumbags were broken open, and the contents splattered over their bound bodies.

Finally, Tom stood over them, looking down. Do you feel as small and weak as I did in the shower, he wondered? He didn't feel sorry for Dobbs, who broke so soon. In fact, he felt vindicated. I am strong, he realized. I'm smart, and I can get what I want, and I lived.

He took hold of his cock and aimed carefully.

They left the room smelling of sweat, cum, and piss.

Will and Tom went home and showered for almost an hour, and fell asleep tangled up in each other.

AFTERWARD

The sign on the gym door simply read CLOSED.
The gates were down, locks in place; and neighborhood residents got used to telling confused-
looking muscular men that they didn't know what
happened, and no, they hadn't heard anything. It
was several weeks before anyone heard anything,
and the only thing that did come out was that the
owner had some kind of emergency to take care
of, and had sold the business. It reopened as a
franchise, with all new fixtures in pastel colors, a
line of stylish designer workout clothes, and a
coed policy.

Tom got a job selling clothing in a fashionable
boutique, thanks to one of Will's friends. His easy
manner and good looks got him a steady clientele
of both men and women, and he made good com-
missions. He joined a gym near the store and
went when he felt like it and did the workouts he

liked to do. He began to go out to different places, to dance clubs and comedy clubs, to pool rooms and sex clubs, and to darkened bars where men gathered to celebrate their masculinity.

It was at one of those places where he bumped into Mike and Dave, his favorite couple from the old gym. The men in the bar wore leather and chains and studs and torn Levis. Dave was all in leather, a big difference from the demure, almost understated look he wore during the day, and Mike was wearing a leather collar and no shirt under his vest. His nipple rings glittered in the darkness. They looked happy to see him and asked him what happened, and he could only tell them that Mr. Marcus had suddenly vanished, and Frank Dobbs with them, and they had not even paid his last paycheck. They made sounds of sympathy, congratulated him on how he was look-ing, and made excuses for going.

"We have to get up early tomorrow," Dave said. "It's my mother's birthday, and we're taking her for lunch."

"Yeah. And this time, let's not forget the flow-ers, sir?"

"Watch your mouth, cum-breath." They laughed together and said farewell.

So that was their secret, Tom thought, as he watched them go. They're into all that SM stuff. He thought about slaves and masters, and being owned, and he thought about mothers. He went home to his lover.

Will was restless these days. He worked irregu-larly, and came home unhappy, and didn't want to talk about it. Sometimes, he would hit the wall or a pillow with his hand and say, "I gotta get out of here!" Tom finally knew what they had to do. Between his new job flipping burgers and Will's mood swings, they had to change something, and soon. He knew that they were still recovering from what happened, like soldiers after the war was done.

"I'm yours, you know," he said, lying in Will's arms the next morning. "No matter what. I belong to you."

"Yeah, I know, Blondie," Will said, hugging him.

"But sometimes I'm afraid. I think you're going to leave me, or that ... or that he'll come back."

Will was silent for a moment. "Yeah, he might. But I'm not going nowhere, Blondie."

"I hated what he did," Tom said softly. "I hated what I thought he made me. But you know, I think I really wasn't ever any different. I still want to be owned, I want to be taken care of. I just want you to do it."

"That's real good to hear, Tom. Real good."

"I gotta make a phone call."

He dialed the number from memory, although it had been months. A woman's voice answered. "Hello, Mom?"

It was so good to hear her voice. Yes, she was surprised to hear from him, but yes, she was very pleased. She was well, so was everyone in the family. No, Dad wasn't home, he was out at the Agway store, buying sweet feed. How was her boy?

"I'm great, Mom, you should see me. I ... I got into bodybuilding, I'm big now, and I have a tan."

"Why that sounds nice, Tom. Are you happy with the way you look?"

"Sure, Mom. But that's not why I called. I

called to tell you something important, Mom, and I really want you to understand that I'm telling you because, um, I love you Mom."

"Yes, Tom? Is everything all right?"

"Yeah. It's just that ... well, I'm gay, Mom."

There was a pause on the other end of the line, and for a moment, Tom thought that his mother had fainted. But her voice came back across the line a second later.

"Was that all of it, Tom? That was the big thing you wanted to tell me?" her voice was very calm, and almost amused.

"But ... uh, yes! Um, I thought, um ..."

"That I didn't know? Honey, we raise a lot of things out this way, but we don't raise a lot of fools. Of course I knew! What kind of a mother would I be if I didn't know my own son?"

"Oh! Well," Tom choked out, blushing a little, "I thought you'd be more, um, upset."

"Now why would I be upset, dear? I know that the Bible says a few things about it, but we all can't be perfect people, we have to live with how we're made. And you're my son, Tom, and I'd love you if you were short, fat and harelipped, as long as you were a good boy and happy with the way you were."

That simple love and wisdom affected Tom deeply, and he talked to his mother for another half-hour before he hung up. He put the phone down and searched the apartment for his address book.

"Now what?" Will asked. He had been amused at Tom's coming-out phone call. "Gonna call all your cousins now?"

"Nope. We're gonna move."

214

"Huh?"

Tom looked up, the address book in his hand. "We need to, Will. If we stay here, we're going to get on each others' nerves and break up soon, I know. I love you, and you love me, but we're too close to ... what happened here. We need to get away, and put it behind us."

"Well, nice of you to ask me, Blondie." But Will did not look like he thought it was such a bad idea. "Where do you wanna move to? Brooklyn?"

"San Francisco."

While Will raised his eyebrows and grinned, Tom dialed the number in his book. In a minute, he got an answer.

"Hello, is Scott there? Yes, tell him it's Tom. Hello? Scott? Hey, guy, how're you doing! Yeah, it's really me! Huh? New York City, chum, the big city! Yeah, I've been here for, hell, almost nine months. Yeah, yeah, I missed you too.

"Listen, I got a favor to ask. I ... I have a lover now.... What? Oh, he's, um, really hot, and really built.... Yeah, and he's here now, so I can't talk." He laughed. "But the thing is, we wanna move out to the West Coast. When? Now! As soon as possible. And I need your help; maybe you can find us a place to stay while we get used to the city, get some new jobs.... What? What do we want to do? Oh, the usual. We want to dress in queer clothes and go to queer clubs and march in queer parades, you know." Tom's voice shook with emotion, and he talked into the phone with an animation that seemed to take all the gloom from the two men and tear it to shreds. Before long, Will was planning what to pack.

$4.95 (CANADA $5.95) • BADBOY

MR. BENSON

041-5

$4.95

M *r. Benson* is the compelling story of a young man's quest for the perfect master and an exacting education in life and sex that only a master can give him. Young Jamie is a lonely clone in the discos of New York, always looking for Mr. Good Bar. Instead, he finds Mr. Benson. Jamie is led down the path of erotic enlightenment by the magnificent Mr. Benson, learning to accept cruelty as love, anguish as affection, and ultimately, this man as his master.

A classic erotic novel from a time when there was no limit to what a man could dream of doing....

"... an SM masterwork. *Mr. Benson* takes its place alongside the classics of the genre."
Samuel Stewart, *Philadelphia Gay News*

"John Preston writes with such white hot intensity that his words have the ability to burn themselves into the erotic unconsciousness."
T.R. Witomski, *The Connection*

"One of the top ten SM novels ever written."
Penthouse

"A classic underground novel."
The Village Voice

"One of the great figures of gay literature ... awesome, forbidding, almost godlike.... He is the ideal Master.... No wonder gay males went out looking for Mr. Benson in droves."
Jesse Monteagudo, *Miami Weekly News*

T E L E N Y

$4.95 (CANADA $5.95) • BADBOY

Often attributed to Oscar Wilde, *Teleny* is a strange, compelling novel, set amidst the color and decadence of *fin-de-siècle* Parisian society. A young stud of independent means seeks only a succession of voluptuous and forbidden pleasures, but instead finds love and tragedy when he becomes embroiled in an underground cult devoted to fulfilling the darkest fantasies.

020-2 $4.95

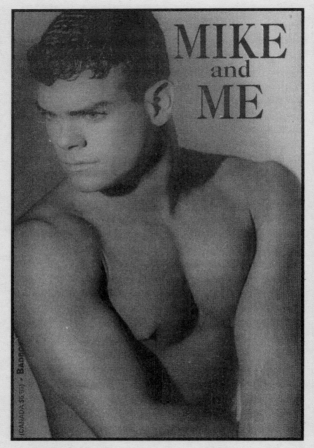

MIKE
and
ME

Mike joined the gym squad at Edison Community College to bulk up on muscle and enjoy the competition. Little did he know he'd be turning on every sexy muscle jock in Southern Minnesota! Hard bodies collide for a series of workouts designed to generate a whole lot more than rips and cuts. Get ready to hit the showers with this delicious muscle-boy fantasy romp!

035-0 **$4.95**

SLOW BURN

Welcome to the Body Shoppe, where men's lives cross in the pursuit of muscle. From the authors who brought you BADBOY's *Men at Work* comes a new anthology of heated obsession and erotic indulgence: *Slow Burn*. Torsos get lean and hard, biceps and shoulders grow firm and thick, pecs widen and stomachs ripple in these sexy stories of the power and perils of physical perfection.

042-3 $4.95

T · H · E

SEXPERT

A collection of
selected columns from
The Advocate Men

EDITED BY
**Pat
Califia**

From the pages of the *Advocate Men*—the hottest gay
men's magazine in the country—comes *The Sexpert*,
the first Badboy nonfiction release.

For many years now, the sophisticated gay man has
known that he can turn to one authority for answers to vir-
tually any question on the subject of man-to-man intimacy
and sexual performance. From penis size to toy care, bar
behavior to AIDS awareness, The Sexpert responds to real
concerns with uncanny wisdom and a razor wit.

This collection of The Sexpert's most outrageous and
useful columns has been edited by Pat Califia, a former
editor of *Advocate Men*.

*Warning: In the interest of of clarity, this book contains
graphic descriptions and strong language.*

Pat Califia's *The Sexpert* is everything you've ever wanted to know about gay sexuality—but never dared to ask.

034-2   **$4.95**

THE HEIR

THE KING

TWO NOVELS by
JOHN PRESTON

John Preston's ground-breaking novel *The Heir*, written in
the lyric voice of the ancient myths, tells the story of a
world where slaves and masters create a new sexual society. Samuel Steward, the author of the classic "Phil Andros"
novels, called *The Heir* "… exciting and gripping, making for
involuntary activity around the groin."

This stylish new edition of the *The Heir* also includes an
ambitious and completely original work by Preston called *The
King*. This epic tale tells the story of a young soldier who dis-
covers his monarch's most secret desires. He uses his body and
his superior knowledge of the sensual arts to capture his king's
body and soul.

The Heir and *The King* demonstrate why *Lambda Book
Report* has called John Preston "The dark lord of gay erotica."

048-2 $4.95

ORDERING IS EASY!

MC/VISA ORDERS CAN BE PLACED BY CALLING OUR TOLL-FREE NUMBER

1-800-458-9640

OR MAIL THE COUPON BELOW TO:

MASQUERADE BOOKS
801 SECOND AVE.,
NEW YORK, N.Y. 10017

MM 028-8

QTY	TITLE	NO.	PRICE
	SUBTOTAL		
	POSTAGE and HANDLING		
	TOTAL		

Add $1.00 Postage and Handling for first book and 50¢ for each additional book. Outside the U.S. add $2.00 for first book, $1.00 for each additional book. New York State residents add 8-$\frac{1}{4}$% sales tax.

NAME _____

ADDRESS _____ **APT #** _____

CITY_____ **STATE**_____ **ZIP** _____

TEL (_____ **)** _____

PAYMENT: ☐CHECK ☐MONEY ORDER ☐VISA ☐MC

CARD NO. _____ **EXP. DATE** _____

PLEASE ALLOW **4-6 WEEKS** DELIVERY. NO C.O.D. ORDERS. PLEASE MAKE ALL CHECKS PAYABLE TO MASQUERADE BOOKS. PAYABLE IN U.S. CURRENCY ONLY.